AMBIVALENT FATES

Noah Hewitt

Noah Hewitt

To my Papa! Robert! To my Uncle! Carlos! To my Uncle! Bill! To my Cousin! Carlito!

Reality is art in of itself. I live and witness each passing moment as if it's all a divine play. It's a poetic, comedic, tragic story. Surely, I'm a part in all of it too. I'd like to be a compelling character myself. One that's very cool!

NOAH HEWITT

CHAPTER 1

Tears of an Angel

December 9, 2050, 4:30 A.M.

The Kremlin Bunker, Moscow, Russia,
The People's Soviet Empire

"Do you love me....?", he muttered.

"Always have, always will", I said.

...

...

...

"Do you forgive me....?", he whimpered.

"Only if you forgive yourself", I said.

...

...

History is cyclical, not linear. Perhaps, that is why humanity found themselves in this circumstance again. But I'll tell you this story, anyway, for it's quite an interesting one, I'll admit. It is, of course, what God ordained to happen, after all, at least in this particular... era in time, at least in this particular world, in this story. So, with that being said, I'll enjoy telling it to you, my ever-so beloved listener, so that you can learn from it, appreciate it, and derive from it a great appreciation for the true poetic art that our God is capable of. For in the headquarters of the Kremlin, there sat the highest-ranking commanders and officers of the People's Soviet Empire, a historic unification of both the modern Russian Federation, and the People's Republic of China, as well as the remaining communist states of the world. A revival of the Soviet Union, with the addition of communist China, North Korea, Cuba, Laos, among others. This monstrously powerful empire consisted of a joint-unification of both the entirety of the modern Russian military, and the full breadth of the Chinese military. Combined, their raw manpower numbered nearly four billion, and their technology and weaponry, having been developed by both the most capable Russian and Chinese engineers and scientists, stood finally in direct competition to the long-lasting technological superiority of the United States.

In this year, 2050, super soldiers and cybernetic, "mech" suits, as well as harnessed-magnetic and nanomachine technology, was utilized widespread by both the West and the East, ushering in a terrifying era of human history, where true monsters walked the earth, in the form of super soldier death squads. These super soldiers resembled most closely to actual ninjas of the antiquated feudal era of Japan, and thus the label, "cyber-ninja", was also commonly used to classify and describe these modern soldiers. They were unfathomably agile, quick, and precise with all their attacks and movements. Melee weapons had also seen a resurrection in the battlefield, with these cyber-ninjas commonly carrying electric as well as magnetically powered blades, for close-quarter-combat. It wasn't just the strength of the blades themselves, but also the ungodly strength and force in which these cyber-ninjas would be able to swing them with, via their super-enhanced arm strength, which resulted in devastating damage.

But alas, the fighting had been mostly finished. And the over-ambitious People's Soviet Empire, commonly known as the P.S.E., had been surrounded by a weaponized and highly emotionally-charged, U.S. led coalition, consisting of soldiers from all of N.A.T.O., the U.N., as well as the rest of the world, that of whom was unified in their opposition to autocratic, communist world domination. Some of the heaviest players in this worldly alliance were the U.S., the U.K., Canada, France, really all of Europe, and the democratic world at large.

Just as World War II had ended, with the Axis forces on their knees, the P.S.E. had overestimated their strength, and had found most of their territory ravaged, and burned, and brutalized by war. Leading this empire was one singular man, who had been responsible for the most deaths in all of human history, consequently from

World War III, which he had directly started, where only the archaic wrathful conquest of Genghis Khan held a candle to his damnation, and casualty count. This man, and his closest advisors and bodyguards, all sat in a deep underground bunker in the Kremlin. They were all mostly terrified, knowing that they had disrespected their mother earth to such an evil extent, having burned the fields, polluted the waters, littered the forests with bloodied bodies and the such. They all, each and every single one of these close, high-ranking officers and advisors, knew they were destined for Hell. However, it was their pride, and their blind submission to their hypnotizing leader, that kept them still invested in their earthly presence, were they not completely oblivious to their demise and utter defeat.

Their Grand Soviet Emperor, whom they, in part of some being initiated into an inner-cult of deification and worship, and for whom they followed to no end, was still smiling, where he sat at the head of the long table, inside the bunker. This singular leader, the Great Leader, was a 51-year-old man named Naydyr Chanming. Naydyr had used highly developed and personalized nanomachine technology to stop, as well as reverse, himself from aging, and thus, he held the appearance of roughly a 25-year-old. This man, Naydyr, had unified Russia and China in large part due to his ability to relate to the core of both nations' peoples. He was, after all, a half Russian, half Chinese man, who spoke both Russian and all varieties of Chinese fluently. Truly, a one of one figure, in all of history, so incredibly unique, regrettably so. Naydyr was gifted with what his inner cult called the "Voice of the Dragon". His impassioned speeches about the nobleness and upstanding justification of communism in the modern age subdued the Russians, especially the jaded, impressionable, and idealistic youth, and put the already accustomed communist Chinese peoples to actual tears, for his words struck such a nerve. You see, Naydyr was the son of a Russian oligarch, an oil and diamond baron. His mother, a Chinese woman, had died during childbirth, perhaps saving her from a life of anguish, being the mother of such an unbridled beast. Naydyr, later in life, and in an effort to better emphasize his Chinese heritage, adopted his deceased mother's surname, Chanming. Many theorized that maybe it was the absence of a mother's love that led to Naydyr's demonic development.

Regardless, Naydyr's decision making proved to have brought both the once glorious nations of Russia and China to complete and utter devastation and destruction for its people. At the long table, where Naydyr and his closest confidants sat, there was only one other man, out of the dozen or so, who knew what would come next.

You see, Naydyr was not so much different from, say, Josef Stalin, who was known to have been terribly paranoid, about everything and anything to do with his duty as leader, which in Naydyr's case, was his official role as "First Citizen of the People's Soviet Empire". Only one other single soul in the bunker knew of Naydyr's next decision, which was to detonate the Dead Man's Hand, a series of secretly hidden nuclear bombs scattered all across the world, thus eviscerating the entire planet, except that of the lands and territories of the P.S.E. The Dead Man's Hand, as they called it, was first implemented as early as the 1950's, only one year after the first public Soviet detonation of a nuclear bomb in 1949. The original

Soviets, back then, of what was now known as the "First Soviet Union" or the "Original Soviet Union", realized that anti-aircraft technology would inevitably become so advanced and efficient that a worldwide nuclear firing of airborne nuclear warheads would, in time, become unrealistic.

Instead, over the course of decades, they planted nuclear bombs in almost every country. Many were underground, some were in inaccessible locations, others were even hidden under, or in, foreign embassies. Quite the incredible feat, one that no tactician could appreciate, for it was secret, even to a vast majority of the Soviet inner-sphere, and the entire P.S.E. populace at large. The U.S. had, in fact, been tipped off about this through their network of spies and informants, but through the elapsing of several decades, it became treated like more of a myth, considered blatant and unrealistic Soviet propaganda. It sounds far-fetched, which is exactly why nobody believed in it being true. It was not out of character, however, for the Soviets, who were known for their simple, pragmatic, practical planning, not unlike an instance such as during the Space Race of the Cold War, where the Soviets opted to use pencils in space as opposed to spending millions developing a space-functioning pen.

The other individual in the bunker who was aware that Naydyr planned on triggering the Dead Man's Hand was his right-hand man, and second-in-command, Ruslan Payurov. A wicked man by any regards, he was a childhood friend of Naydyr's. Naydyr and Ruslan had quite the meteoric rise, growing up, and they were deathly loyal to each other.

Security screens in the bunker room showed U.S.

super soldier death squads approaching the premises. Naydyr made eye contact with Ruslan, and Ruslan returned him a simple nod. A nod of approval, and deep understanding. Naydyr then looked over at the men who sat at this long table, and he had no respect for any of them. To him, they were puny fools, because their destinies were not that important, in Naydyr's eyes. This imbalance was a direct contrast to the unhealthy dedication and lofty idolization each of these high-ranking officers felt towards Naydyr. It was as if their submission was contrasted with disrespect. And thus, Naydyr stood up from the table. All the P.S.E. officers didn't know what he would do next, but Ruslan smirked slyly and looked at the ground.

"God, forgive me, that is, if you still have the heart to hear me", Ruslan muttered under his breath.

Naydyr, then, with exceptional grace, placed one foot on the table, and climbed up on top of it. You must understand, the detonation button for the Dead Man's Hand was directly in front of him, on the table. The rest of the P.S.E. officers were beginning to understand what was about to happen, and a combination of dread, terror, and regret filled their souls. You must not forget; these were human beings too. Naydyr then, rather ominously, stood directly straight, erected upward, atop the table, with his left foot placed just inches from the button. It was his designer shoes that would spell the end for mother earth. Naydyr, was after all, the emperor of a communist empire, but he himself, having attended privileged and exclusive American boarding schools in his youth, had been known to have developed a taste for capitalistic, luxurious items and brands. He was also a hypocrite.

The only thing crossing Naydyr's mind... was how his name would ring in infamy for generations to come, not only on earth, but in the eons of time, immortalized in this reality's timeline as the Great Destroyer. Naydyr looked down at the button. He felt high. Elated, that he had really become so insurmountably capable of such a historical power. He had not conquered the world as he sought to, but if he could not accomplish that, then he assuredly would leave a permanent mark on it. A scar, a blemish. Nobody else, perhaps forever, would ever get the chance to do what he couldn't.

In the depths of his soul, Naydyr mused to himself, "I didn't come this far, just to come this far."

One of the officers, then in a moment of impulsive vindication, perhaps to save face in light of his ancestors watching, and for his family, who he had been thinking about, leaped out of the table and lunged at Naydyr, accompanied with a single scream, "Glory to the Russian Federation!" It was an unfortunate event, because Ruslan then pulled out his personalized Russian handgun, and shot him dead, almost immediately, before he could make his way to stop what was about to happen. Naydyr did not even look in his direction, for he was so enveloped in his own mind, he was actually, in that moment, conscious of something else entirely, replaying a music video he had filmed in his mind during this whole ordeal. Naydyr, had, yes, filmed a number of music videos, for in his time attending school in America, he developed a love for the American music scene, and sought to imitate it, as sort of a passion project of his. Regardless, Naydyr then spread his arms out in a messiah-like pose, standing straight and erect on the table, and said his own little prayer.

"I know you would be proud, friend", said Naydyr softly, as he then looked down at the detonation button, which seemed so especially vulnerable, ever so small and tiny. Surely remarkable, Ruslan thought to himself, how such a tiny machination could render such gigantic effects. But who was this "friend" that Naydyr was referring to? Only Ruslan knew, for he was referring to the devil himself, Satan. Yes, it was so regrettably true, that Naydyr idealized himself, in his own warped, disturbed mind, as the representation of the devil himself, a second, and future, counterpart to the holy Jesus himself, who was understood to be the representative of God. There was simply put, no limit to how important Naydyr viewed himself, and seemingly no hope for forgiveness.

"I have seen the end many times", said Naydyr. Even Ruslan did not know what he meant by this remark, but what did it matter?

And alas, all the wicked spirits and souls who were doomed to roam the earth, for they were unfit to join heaven, gathered around the scene, eating their popcorn, so to speak, watching in great anticipation. Nobody in the room could see them, though, of course, and only Naydyr and Ruslan were conscious of their presence. And with the climax and "beat drop" of Naydyr's own music building up, playing in his head, Naydyr raised his left leg. Ruslan noticed that Naydyr had chosen to step on the detonation button with his left leg, and wondered, could this be his friend's ultimate subscription to the Left Hand Path? The Left Hand Path, the selfish and evil path, opposite of the just and noble Right Hand Path, for Ruslan had grown to never put any minor detail past his companion, who he knew to be ever-so conscious of these spiritual tenets. The officers were absolutely frozen. Having just witnessed one of their fellow officers shot and murdered, they then understood that this was a matter completely unbeknownst to them, this was Naydyr and Ruslan's matter. It was unfortunate, and rather shameful, as many of the surrounding spirits, chattering amongst themselves, reasoned that if all of them together rushed Naydyr and Ruslan, they could have potentially overpowered both of these Two Beasts. But they didn't. And consequently, they would be known as the greatest cowards that ever lived, having failed all of humanity, in the short window that they could've stopped this madness.

Naydyr looked out into the air, the space in front of him, and Ruslan wondered, what did he see, what was he looking at? But in his heart, he knew ever so clearly, for he was fantasizing in his head, in his accursed seat of consciousness, fantasizing of the Armageddon, the final cherry-on-top, of his long tenured career of wrath. And when the song in Naydyr's head reached its highest point, Naydyr stamped down his designer shoe, on the detonation button, and so much of the entire world was instantly eviscerated within twenty seconds, save for the lands of the Soviet Kingdom.

And the angels' wept.

CHAPTER 2

Wanted Dead

December 9, 2050, 5:05 A.M.

The Kremlin Bunker, and Roof, Moscow,
Russia, The People's Soviet Empire

Over 13 billion of the world's then 15 billion people were instantly eviscerated, vaporized, so terribly murdered. It was then, of course, that Naydyr and Ruslan knew they very desperately had to leave, immediately. Naydyr, rather satisfied with himself, hopped off the table, all while simultaneously, and with incredible force, an explosion close to the bunker went off, near the locked entrance. The American-led N.A.T.O. and U.N. death squad had arrived. These American super soldiers were not clones, but they were genetically, cybernetically, and mentally enhanced, in many, many ways. As mentioned before, they most closely resembled ninjas; futuristic, dystopian, killing-machine ninjas. But alas, their cause was noble. They fought for freedom... which had now turned to revenge.

"Visitors", muttered Ruslan.

"Time to dance, baby", Naydyr said softly. He then smiled slightly, as he pulled out a machine pistol, a rapid firing, compact firearm, that Naydyr kept strapped against him at all times, which it had finally seen a time to shine.

You must also know, you see, that Naydyr was also a whimsical, lighthearted man. He could be deathly serious, and equally intimidating, in his fiery speeches, but also casually complacent, even in the face of an assassination attempt. This was because, as Ruslan had grown to understand, Naydyr truly and utterly believed with his entire ounce of being that he was divinely protected, and simply a puppet of fate. He did not believe in free-will, he felt that was a foolish, naïve weakness to subscribe to. He did not fear death, either. He only feared his inability to live up to his destiny, one that he had decided for himself, in part, but also didn't completely take credit for, as he felt ordained, or chosen, so to speak. Selected, that is, by both God and Satan themselves.

But alas, these N.A.T.O. and U.N. soldiers attempting to enter the bunker were the ultimate killing machines, of all ages, only the famed Spartans of Leonidas held a candle to them. They had, after all, slashed and decimated through hordes of the last remaining P.S.E. defenses, having penetrated deep into the heartland of the empire, Moscow. And they were on a shoot-on-sight protocol, for this was the absolute peak, and hopeful conclusion, of World War III, and to hold Naydyr accountable in a trial was simply a naïve, foolish, even silly cause. He would just be sentenced to death anyway, for war crimes, and it didn't help that their communications base for whom served as their intel was just destroyed back in America. They understood, this band of brothers and sisters, that it was up to them, no one else, and they might not ever get a second chance to achieve justice for their mother earth, their mother countries, and of course, their murdered families. This task force was spearheaded by the two most dangerous and skilled super soldiers of the entire Western forces, a French woman, named Joy Adelyn, and an American man, Raven Leverette. Joy had become the most decorated soldier in modern combat history, responsible for over 10,000 individual confirmed kills, consisting mostly of P.S.E. ground-soldiers, and her weapons of choice were a modified, modernized European double-edged longsword, altered with a supersonic, ultra-sharp, sonically-charged blade, capable of easily cutting through even tanks, let alone the flimsy flesh of a P.S.E. brute, coupled with a suppressed, and fully-automatic, assault rifle that also had its own laser beam attachment, for aiming, and specialized sighting. It is worth noting, honestly, that the 10,000 death tallies to her name may seem extrapolated or exaggerated, but you must understand, this conflict had been ongoing for over an entire decade, and the face of war was drastically different, with individual super soldiers capable of unprecedented damage all on their own, let alone Joy, who was the most elite of them all.

Raven, over intercom to the death squad, said sharply, "Don't shoot him in the head, I want his face untouched. I want his severed head on display in my office."

"That goes especially for you, Adelyn," he added.

Joy had, after all, held the record for most "headshots" amongst the death squad.

All Joy could think about then was how all the Americans and French citizens were vaporized so needlessly and wastefully, and a single tear shed from her face. Joy had always been an empath, inside, quite ironically contrasting her outer, natural-born-killer appearance.

"Hate to break it to you but your office is long gone, Leverette", chimed back Joy.

They were on the other side of the bunker now, and with an explosive, a modernized and incredibly destructive, futuristic and highly classified explosive, the bunker door was then blown open. It was then, that Naydyr, on the opposite side of the room, unpinned several grenades from his chest and waist, letting them drop to the floor, from where he then kicked them each all at once, with the tip of his designer shoe, across the room to where Joy, Raven, and the rest of the death squad were. A singular move that was impossibly executed with the most specific of graces, which impressed Ruslan considerably. When these grenades exploded, they also doubled as heavy smoke grenades. Naydyr and Ruslan escaped then through a backdoor, at their opposite side of the room, and stepped onto a highly advanced, magnetically-charged elevator platform, rapidly ascending to the highest roof of the Kremlin, from which they came from the most bottom level of the building, where this bunker had resided.

Naydyr and Ruslan's personalized mech suits were waiting for them, on the roof.

They planned to use them to fly away.

Their escape wasn't met without whizzing bullets however, as Joy and Raven and the rest of the death squad were in fact able to catch a glimpse of them, rushing out the back exit and into the elevator. Very quickly, Joy entered her mental, warrior-state of "kill-mode", and Raven used his bionic legs, a feature of his cybernetic super soldier suit, to leap across the room to where the elevator was. Raven gazed upward, watching the fading silhouettes of the two men... that had just set ablaze to the whole world. Joy rushed next to Raven.

They even made brief eye contact, Naydyr and Joy, and Joy instantly felt an ever-penetrating voice and sudden jolt to her system. As Naydyr glanced back, he unloaded and sprayed his rapid firing pistol at them. Raven and Joy both sidestepped out of the line of fire.

"Joy, it's Joan", spoke a deeply powerful, almost angelic, and ancient sounding voice.

Joy, having stepped aside, felt this familiar presence in her soul, when she heard this voice in her head. She knew she wasn't schizophrenic, for not being so was a necessary aspect to the screening process of joining her numerous, highly classified, super-elite black operations, and this voice wasn't from the intercom that her and her fellow death squad shared. No, it was a direct, intangible, otherworldly voice, that spoke from directly within her, to her. A voice, she then reasoned and paraded in her head, that must've been that of an angel, or even God himself. All the while that this was happening to Joy, she saw the now distant silhouettes of Naydyr and Ruslan fade even farther up the elevator shaft, as their platform elevated away, into the distance.

"You can't lose them!", the permeating, powerful voice then said, in her head.

Joy knew she wasn't crazy. In fact, Joy was the farthest from it, she was in an absolute peak mental, physical, and emotional condition, a necessary result of her extensive training, the harshest and most demanding offered in the entire world at large, military or not. This was a direct communication with the spirit world, she then quickly understood. But... "Joan", who was this "Joan"?

I guess, I'll let you know, for it was Joan of Arc, the famous historical French heroine, who was a hero of the battlefield in the 15th century, having accomplished a number of integral French victories during the Hundred Years War.

It was because Naydyr's nuclear holocaust was so forcefully immense, that it shattered the barrier between the tangible, physical, "real" world, and that of the invisible, esoteric, "spirit" world. And thus, for those who were important enough, those who would be the most receptive, who were at a suitable enough point in their spiritual development, the spirits, or consciousnesses, of their past life would then reach out to them, in the form of a simple voice, a familiar, yet unfamiliar, voice. Joy Adelyn, once a French woman of humble origins, the now famed great "Ghost of France", the greatest sniper, soldier, and heroine in modern combat history, was indeed, the famed Joan of Arc, reincarnated.

If history is truly cyclical, not linear, then one could deduce that yes, momentous figures in history then live again, being reborn, physically, only because their time on earth wasn't entirely finished yet, for they had not yet achieved their soul's ultimate destiny. These destinies, of course, vary from person to person, and not everyone on earth goes through as many reincarnations as others do. But for those special, inspiring, typically historically prominent figures, such a Joan of Arc, their ambitious souls often are tasked, from God himself, to take the accomplishments and lessons learned in their legendary lifespans, and to "go back" to earth, often to lead, to lead those with lesser destinies, who can't lead themselves.

"Joy, God assigns his strongest soldiers with his hardest jobs, after all, isn't that what they say, in English? Something like that. Joy, I'm Joan, Joan of Arc, I'm your past life. And I'm making contact with you so that we can accomplish this together, for France, and for the world."

"Joy, I'm so proud of you. Joy, you could never know, just how much love I have for you, my little girl, my warrior."

Joy, hearing this, and immediately understanding in her soul, that this was true, and really happening to her, shed another, single tear. For Joy, it was quite remarkable, given how many other people she had mercilessly slain and killed, having persisted through this lifestyle of alienating carnage, that there was someone else, someone she had known all her life, without knowing it, that completely and utterly understood her, who loved her more purely and honestly than any other one person could even hope to come close too. For who could love and understand oneself... more than oneself?

"Don't worry, Joan. This one's for France", Joy thought in her head, assuming that was the way to communicate back to Joan. She didn't know if Raven also had his past life make contact with him or not, but she didn't think so, for she knew him to not be as spiritually receptive to those types of things, he more so fit the cold, stoic, jaded, grizzled soldier archetype. She wasn't even sure if Raven believed in God, either. She didn't blame him, though, for it did occur to her that they had both lived through enough human monstrosities to surely encourage doubt in the existence of any all-encompassing, benevolent figure. However, she considered this a misdirection of emotion, a character flaw of his, that the suffering of life did not bring him closer to Source, to God, but rather pushed him away from it. But, then again, she couldn't blame him. For she, quite literally, had any doubt in God or reincarnation directly evaporated, having finally made contact with Joan. He simply could never understand, unless it happened to him too, which it visibly had not, at least not yet. But regardless, this ushered a sense of euphoric elation, inside the deepest depths of her being, for she knew she would never be alone again, she would never feel the way she felt, before, during her lifetime of lonely years. It occurred to her... "Joan of Arc" ... "Joy Adelyn" ... both names resembled each other, phonetically and vowelly. She had to chuckle to herself, God had a sense of humor too.

Joan whispered, "Go. Go make me proud. Go do what you were born to do." And Joy, having fired a shootable zipline attached to her right arm, ascended up the elevator shaft. She clutched her longsword tightly, shooting upward, ready to slice Naydyr and Ruslan both in half, that was if she could reach them before they flew away in their mechs.

Having finally reached the roof of the Kremlin, the absolute highest point of the Kremlin, atop where additional levels had been built, were both mechs, waiting. These mechs had many interesting features, and each had cost roughly a trillion dollars each to engineer, create, and personalize. For one, both mechs were not as large as one may think, for a mobile, agile, seamless and streamlined design was heavily emphasized in their creation. Upon stepping into the mech, Naydyr's height was increased, say, from 6'2" in shoes to about 7'0", even. So, they weren't exactly just simply a suit of superpowered armor, like the cyber-ninja suits that Joy, Raven, and the death squad wore, but rather, they were pronouncedly a step above. However, they still retained the speed and dexterity of these less adorned cyber-ninja suits, actually more so, because they featured more advanced technology and possessed a higher capacity for force generation, in both the legs, feet, hands, and arms. These mechs were also adorned with anti-gravity technology, not the traditionally mass-produced jetpacks that your average super soldier or cyber-ninja was equipped with. So yes, these were quite literally floating, ultimate, trillion-dollar death machines. They were intended most deservedly for the men who sold away the whole world, to then defend themselves... against the whole world.

Each mech had an interestingly important aesthetical design to them, most notable in the mask, helmet, or "face", of each respective mech. The face of Naydyr's mech, that covered and protected his own face, was modeled closely after a particular person from history, of whom Naydyr personally worshiped and dedicated most of his wicked deeds to, in the name of this man's memory. This was, of course, a Roman emperor, specifically the infamous fifth Roman emperor of the original Julio-Claudian dynasty, Nero Caesar, also known as Neron, or simply, Nero. For you must understand this very importantly, in the same exact way in which Joan had contacted Joy, ushering in a synergetic unification of current life and past life, Naydyr had already accomplished that many, many decades earlier. It was actually his best kept secret. Naydyr had delved into the occult and esoteric teachings so heavily that he had, in quite literally the most serious of terms, communicated already with a whole host of spirits, and demons, and in which this accursed roster of higher-dimensional consciousnesses had then actually taken a liking to him. They bestowed both transcendental knowledge upon him, both about his destiny and his own past life. As a result, Naydyr had his personalized mech fitted with a mask that was modeled most closely after the traditional depiction of Nero's face, drawing inspiration from the classic Roman busts of Nero. This meant that the mask of Naydyr's mech was complete with an especially fat neck, accentuated, manically intense eyes, a bloated, circular, round face, indicative of Cushing's disease, and all the other classically held traits of Nero's appearance, described throughout the ages by Roman scribes, such as that of Suetonius. As you may have deduced, it was true, then, that Naydyr was Nero in his past life, and as Nero had supposedly set fire to Rome, Naydyr had set fire to the world. In the same way that Joan had achieved victory for France, and Joy was to achieve victory for the world, evil souls and evil consciousnesses also had their own evil destinies and plans as well.

Thus, Naydyr, a deeply nostalgic and sentimental man, had many Neronian features to his mech. The number "666" was inscribed, carved into the metal that ran across his mask's forehead, on Nero's recreated metal face. And for those uninitiated, or unenlightened, the deeply meaningful value of 666 had been long paraded as being the "Devil's number" in pop-culture for so many decades, but it actually had a much more specific, and exact meaning. You see, the number 666 was actually a codeword for the name "Nero". This name was referred to within the Book of Revelations, the last book of the bible, though the usage of 666. And this 666 being the "Number of a Man", or the "Number of the Beast", was really referring to Nero, not the devil or Satan. This is because when the Apostle John, who was banished to the remote island of Patmos, for being a Christian in the early era of the Roman Empire, aimed to write and warn the other Christians of Nero's wrath, he knew he could not use Nero's literal name, "Nero", so freely and liberally. For his work, the Book of Revelations, would most likely be destroyed or cast away, as it would be considered defamation of the emperor's name, a crime of high treason that would jeopardize the survival of his work.

So, in place, the Apostle John wrote of the man who bore the number "666", the number of the "Beast", which of course he intended to be understood as "Nero" to his fellow Christians. Nero, was, after all, the first figure in history to persecute Christians, so it was to be understood who the Apostle John was referring to, almost naturally, at the time to other Christians. But this obvious meaning was of course lost in time, like so many other ancient translations, warnings, and teachings.

Now where scholars, historians, theologians, archaeologists of the ancient scriptures, and biblical experts altogether contest each other and engage in their own personal conjecture, is whether the Apostle John employed 666 to either allude to Nero himself, or a future reincarnation of Nero. For the terrible wrath of the "Man who bore the number 666 on his forehead", that the Apostle John described, could be understood both as either the original Nero, and his genocidal treatment of the Christians, or that of a future Nero who would return to earth, "From the bottom of nations", to have his revenge. Deeply insidious, yet interesting, stuff, I know.

It was the latter philosophy, the one which purported 666 to refer to Nero's second life, that Naydyr subscribed to, for he believed himself to be that very person that was being referred to. Yes, you understood that correctly… Naydyr viewed himself as a biblically predicted phenomenon of the future… and he most certainly, in his own eyes, had lived up to the legend. But, none of this was too important to him, as he had accepted this to be his essence and destiny for many long decades by now, and it didn't mean too much to him, admittedly, anymore. Naydyr was really more engaged in being present in the moment, living and experiencing his own legend, than he was being mindful of his past life, or anything or the sort.

That's not to say that he wasn't in direct contact with the original Nero, in his head, however. Which he was, just as similar to how Joy had just been, with Joan. It's just that Naydyr had accomplished this communication, again, for so many decades now, that it was nothing new to him. And this was of course, a highly glossed over and largely unknown fact, that the People's Soviet Empire's Great Leader had a literal evil voice in the back of his mind, for how could anyone else know, or tell? Harkening back to my mentioning of a deeper, inner-circle, cult that revolved around Naydyr, only those members truly knew who Naydyr really listened to, who he really took advice from, who he really respected. "Nero Caesar", "Naydyr Chanming". It was in the similarity of the names' very makeup, the obviousness of who he really was, or so at least that's what was taught in Naydyr's Neronian cult.

"Such a beautiful piece of true Soviet engineering... I know not how long I'll enter you... or when I'll have to depart from you... but oh how beautiful you came out to be", Naydyr said softly, as he stepped into it, entering his demonic suit of metal, letting it read his body-temperature, calibrate to his vitals, and prime its weaponry.

So evidently, it was apparent that Naydyr took great joy in the customization of his mech, with its 666 branding and its Neronian visage. Nero, was after all, known for being obsessed with the arts, having disregarded his duty as emperor in place of his artistic endeavors. Ruslan as well, much to the encouragement of Naydyr, took his time personalizing his respective mech too, during its creation.

Ruslan's mech was adorned with many geometric patterns, etched into the metal. These geometric designs were of course, darkly occult in nature, being occult geometry, and were indicative of a practitioner of mysticism, specifically Eastern mysticism, as well as purely evil witchcraft, of the Eastern schools of black magic. His helmet, or mask, was complete with the design of a heavy beard, and thick mustache.

This was because "Ruslan Payurov" ... was the reincarnation of Rasputin.

Rasputin, yes, the infamous and equally mysterious Russian mystic and self-proclaimed holy man, a certified warlock by any account, who cozied up to the last of the royal Russian dynasty, the Romanovs, and whose presence almost certainly cursed them as well, resulting in their fate of being bayoneted to death by the Bolsheviks. It was as if their brutal deaths were judicially ordered, by God himself, for having housed and welcomed such a deeply Satanic, and dark, evil man.

Naydyr Chanming and Ruslan Payurov, best friends and comrades, who in their previous lives were none other than the two most damned men who perhaps ever lived, Nero and Rasputin.

For Ruslan, also, with the help and aid of Naydyr's spiritual mental teachings and exercises, was also able to "connect" with the consciousness of his previous life, being Rasputin's, and he was also constantly in dialogue with his past life, similar to what Joy had just achieved.

But unlike the newly rebirthed Joy, and more so in the same vein as Naydyr, Ruslan had established this spiritual, synergetic relationship many, many decades ago.

That was one of the very many reasons that Naydyr and Ruslan did not speak too much, especially in the case of Naydyr, who, save for his grand propaganda speeches, spoke softly more times than not, always cultivating an inner, silent peace within himself, taking direction and conversing with Nero.

"Get in the mech you damn beautiful superstar", bellowed Nero, in Naydyr's head.

I can't make this up, but I guess, rather hilariously, Nero and Naydyr cracked each other up... pretty much all day, every day, and had for the past several decades, since the very first exchange between the two separate consciousnesses.

"What did you think of my performance there, when I set ablaze to this forsaken world?" Naydyr replied to Nero, in his head, as his mech wrapped around his limbs, securing himself inside, underneath the layers of Siberian graphene, an even harder and more mobile version of traditional graphene, which was already tougher than diamond.

"Let's see who gets more kills, you or Ruslan."

"Don't embarrass me in front of Rasputin", muttered Nero.

Ruslan, on the other hand, had become enveloped by his mech as well. He was having his own conversations with Rasputin in his own mind too, and together, along with Naydyr, the four consciousnesses overlooked the battlefield, in front of the Kremlin. Naydyr and Ruslan together stood atop this highest point of the Kremlin like vultures looking down, and they could see the tanks, and armies of N.A.T.O. and U.N. soldiers, coming their way, and yet, they both felt exhilarated, especially Naydyr. Naydyr, who was, as mentioned before, someone who had quite perversely been in love with American music, capitalism, and luxury, had a music player built into his mech's interface, and you can bet that it was playing some of his favorite music. It was then that Ruslan motioned to Naydyr a thumbs down, signaling that they ought to both jump off the roof and make their grand escape, away from this all, most especially with Joy and Raven's company shortly following them.

"Get that fat glutton to jump off already, Ruslan", spoke Rasputin in an indignant voice. Whereas Nero was always lightening the mood with his sarcasm, humor, and uniquely dark sense of outgoingness, Rasputin was notably drearier. He was, after all, a monk, compared to that of Nero, who was a spoiled emperor. Rasputin was the colder, more restrained, more succinct voice, when compared to the boisterous, uninhibited persona that Nero carried. And perhaps, almost naturally, Naydyr and Ruslan both reflected these characteristics as well, Naydyr was the more talkative one while Ruslan was more introspective, sparsely displaying emotion.

"They're they are, strike them!" rang the war-cry of Joan in Joy's mind.

It was then, after just a few moments of Naydyr and Ruslan calibrating themselves into their mechs, that Joy emerged from the elevator shaft, which had been over thirty floors, numbering ten more than the original twenty floors of the Kremlin, for the P.S.E. had expanded upon the building considerably over the last decade, both for defense and intelligence purposes. Naydyr rotated his mechanical helm and took one glance at her, and with Ruslan, they both hopped off the edge of the roof, and descended downward, reaching terminal velocity quickly as they each nosedived towards the ground.

"That stupid, worthless pawn of fate. She doesn't understand her destiny is below yours, below ours", denoted Nero in the back of Naydyr's head, with an immense flavor of hatred and disgust. Nero, was, after all, a very deprived, disturbed person, both in his physical life and seemingly even more so in his afterlife, where he counseled Naydyr. Conceivably, this was most narcissistic, because Nero knew his audience, now, when expressing himself was... just another very version of himself, Naydyr.

While Naydyr and Ruslan were both nosediving, they each released a flurry of incredibly destructive, miniature explosives, more precisely being describable as "sticky" grenades. Just before making contact with the battlefield ground, all these sticky grenades were then projected outward via a gust of air, stemming from the very mechanisms that primed them ready to explode. Naydyr and Ruslan then, simultaneously, engaged their anti-gravity propulsion technology, and just several meters from hitting the ground, exploded upwards and forwards, most comparable to a sharp, right angle, and with a generated, but controlled, force. They then shot out, at a speed not unlike that of stories of UFO's, capable of making the sharpest, most exacted turns and maneuvers at the stop of a dime, bending and breaking the then seemingly inapplicable laws of airflight. Many of the N.A.T.O and U.N. soldiers had been grossly ripped to shreds from the shrapnel of the sticky grenades, that had spread a great distance, having been additionally pushed out with the momentum of each mech's takeoff. And the soldiers who weren't killed could barely even hope to aim and shoot at these two, which were then just a pair of black blurs. Joy and Raven ran to the edge of the rooftop where these Two Beasts had just descended from, and realizing they did not have the able means to follow them, had to let them go.

It was then, perhaps lightening the mood of desperation and disappointment, that Joy's intercom picked up a signal from another end, which surprised her, for they had assumed America, and the Western world at large, was baptized in radioactive fire.

It was Alaric Georgi, the then 51st President of the United States, and his vice president, Henry Cursor.

"Joy, this is Alaric. I'm going to speak very quickly. I have made contact with Alexander the Great, my past life. Henry has also made contact with Hercules, which is his past life. I was informed from Henry, and Alexander, that you are Joan of Arc, Joy. I'm not sure if Raven has made contact yet, but I don't think so. We all know he doesn't believe in God, so I don't think his past life would shock him like that, just yet. He's not ready, which is why I'm speaking with you, not him. I've cut off his intercom from this transmission. Anyways, we managed to survive the nuclear holocaust, but our lands are ravaged, and our armies are gone."

Joy quickly, and in a muffled manner, voiced back, "Mr. President, I know. Do you know where Naydyr and Ruslan are heading?"

"They are heading for Siberia. There is an underground tunnel there that supposedly leads to an entrance to the Hollow Earth, running upwards past the North Pole", explained Alaric, in a hurried, slightly panicked voice.

It occurred to Joy, that while she knew Alaric, and Henry, both believed in God and spirits and that sort of thing, it still must've been a shocking revelation to them, that is when they made "contact".

"Joy, Henry and I are in a submarine right now. We will meet you at the east coast of Siberia, we are coming from the Alaskan coast. We have weapons. It appears the Soviets did not have any nuclear warheads in the oceans, which is how we survived. We will get them, Joy. I'll be in touch. One last thing… I love you, and I'm glad you're alive… over."

And with a newfound purpose, Joy looked at Raven, and back at the few members of the death squad that had managed to remain, and who had accompanied them for so long, being legends in their own right.

She was to kill Naydyr. Kill Ruslan. It was that simple.

"If they reach it, we may never see them again. They will not return, for they consider themselves done here", articulated Joan.

It was true.

Naydyr and Ruslan zipped through their war-torn, destroyed city, Moscow. But in comparison to the rest of the inflamed world, it was pretty.

"I'll kill them", Joy promised to Joan.

"They're as good as dead."

Tears flowed down the side of her face

CHAPTER 3

Love is in the Air

June 9th, 2036, 11:11 P.M.

Private Reception, Sanya, China, The People's Soviet Empire

"You know I love you; you know that?", Naydyr said with the most charismatic of dispositions, almost like a serpent.

"I love you too, my strong husband, our great leader", replied Pei Peizhi.

Now allow me to take you back some very many years... and humanize our dearest Naydyr Chanming, everyone's favorite, just a little bit, for before our very God, he was just another human, after all.

He was, after all, in this stage of the P.S.E.'s history, more so describable as a visionary leader of the new age; with interesting, clever solutions for many of the world's problems, having possessed a relatable and endearing personality, and with over half the entirety of both the world's population and landmass under his direct control and influence, people all over the world couldn't help but discuss him. He was, by all accounts, someone with an incalculably astronomical net worth, and for this he was also equally famous in the Western world, a place that had grown to become obsessively enamored with successful, wealthy, influential individuals, most likely stemming from their long-since adopted, and evolved, perversion of late-stage capitalism.

Pei Peizhi was in fact the very special woman that Naydyr Chanming had fallen in love with, oh so dearly, and terribly, and for which he had just married, in the most extravagant and illustrious of celebrations, right on the Chinese island of Sanya, considered by many as one of the most romantic places in China, let alone all of the P.S.E., and really the whole world at large, as of recently. In recent years, it had rivaled even Paris, France, as a capital synonymous with love, and tenderness. This was in part because of the construction of numerous luxury resorts, as well as the implementation of shopping districts, high-end dining options, and of course, P.S.E. parks, monuments, and statues, which honored the several heroes and heroines of the young history of the P.S.E., which was already very rich, and therefore a truly inspiring, emotional setting had been established. The placemaking employed here was in fact highly effective, as Sanya grew to be one of the hottest and trendiest tourist destinations in the P.S.E. It was, what Naydyr called it, the "Destination of Lovers."

"You look so handsome today", Pei whispered into Naydyr's ear, for they were romantically, intimately slow-dancing in the center of the gigantic reception hall, for which the highest ranking and prominent P.S.E. generals, officers, advisors, and statesmen were all watching closely, almost possessed. No one dared disrespect the Great Leader and his chosen Queen, even if that meant not paying attention to them. Displayed readily visible in the foreground of the room were two gigantic portraits of both Naydyr and Pei, akin to Mao's famous portrait, and make no mistake, there was of course the iconic golden hammer and sickle propped proudly behind these portraits.

Pei, was, by any account, a woman most befitting of Naydyr, in many respects, for Naydyr, not unlike that of his predecessor Nero, had had his fair share of affairs, and instances of hypersexuality and overall degeneracy when it came to women. Not as bad, though, as Nero, but still admittedly notable. Regardless, it was at the point in Naydyr's life that he felt he should "settle down", and Pei was a true superstar, an international icon, in every sense of the word. For she was actually the highest streamed, listened to, and shared female musical artist in the entire world, and this was in part due to a very intricately concerted effort, a psychological operation, by the P.S.E. in an attempt to dominate the music industry, and resultantly penetrate yet another aspect of the Western world. As in the same way, from the beginning of the early 2010's all the way into the duration of the 2020's, that South Korean pop music had seen a meteoric, abounding rise in the Western world, having already tightened its grip on the Asian sphere, the P.S.E. was heavily inspired by this phenomenon. And if you have learned anything by now, it's that you never put anything past the minds of obsessive communists, quite frankly, and simply, and the P.S.E. wanted to pivot the focus from "K-Pop", to "C-Pop", ushering a newly created era of Chinese pop music that would mimic the world's love for K-Pop.

This was a highly swift and successful psychological operation. Pei Peizhi had become what even the most lauded and obsessed over K-Pop idols could ever even hope to achieve.

There were many factors to this. Firstly, the P.S.E was composed of the full Chinese population, which numbered close to three billion as the 2020's came to a close, as well as that of the complete Russian and classical Soviet satellite states, which was another 450 million or so people. So, quite evidently, Pei had the sheer numbers on her side, such as social media likes, video views, music streams, all the things that come with having a fanbase numbering well over billions. And yes, Pei's music was actually half decent as well! You see, the P.S.E. conducted a several years long study on some of the biggest hits in K-Pop history over its peak duration of popularity, as a genre. What these P.S.E. psychologists and human-behavior experts, coupled with the most veteran of songwriters, deduced was that a simple chorus that could also be understood in English was of paramount importance. The second tenet in which P.S.E. researchers then understood to be paramount was the inclusion of something that was, diametrically complementary to the familiarity of the English, a reference to something native of Asia. Listeners would then have their interest peaked, and would expectedly look up what the Asian reference meant, wanting to understand what was conveyed to them as "exotically foreign", as P.S.E. researchers dubbed it. As you can see, the P.S.E. was highly manipulative, obsessively ambitious and controlling, and had forcefully pushed Pei as their superstar to all reaches of their empire, and the rest of the world at large. They succeeded.

Pei's own personal biggest hit was of course the smash single, "Shanghai Way". Perhaps quite embarrassingly and even shamelessly, Shanghai Way was almost a rather soulless song, being an engineered propaganda anthem, as it was best understood, from a largely-detached viewpoint. It proved not to matter, though. Shanghai Way surpassed all the most popular songs in internet history in views and streams quite inevitably, which was also in part because the Soviet State, as was tradition of the Russian cyber-unit in the past, utilized an almost unfathomable number of fake accounts, bots, fake likes, shares, reposts, and all of the sort. Shanghai Way had garnered 36 billion views on YouTube by the year 2036, incomprehensibly so.

Pei's legacy as a performer and artist, was then of course, somewhat polarizing. She was both authentically worshiped by billions of rabid fans from the all-expansive, overwhelming P.S.E. landmass, but there was still also a sizable portion of online support that was actually fake accounts and bots, and in the West, she was seen as a propaganda piece by critics and detractors who were the wiser. But the numbers were still the numbers, and when you or whoever logged online, you saw her face, and her clout, and there was nothing you could do about it.

It is also worth mentioning that Pei had been an on-and-off lover and mistress of Naydyr for many years, throughout her career, and his, and although it was never admitted, many knowledgeable of the C-Pop psychological operation reasoned that Naydyr had specifically chosen Pei as his championess, the benefactor of this massive government effort.

"You know I just want to give you the whole world, Pei. Everything, and anything, all for you, it's only us, Pei", whispered back Naydyr, while the two continued to slow-dance.

This was actually true. And Pei knew it. Just another reason for her to have been so loyal to him. He, in a way, had made her, he was her secret promoter, behind the scenes, pulling all the strings to boost her. When you would think of the greatest performers in music history, you would mention the names of the greats, and now Pei Peizhi, too.

"I have to say, your version of Poppaea does rival my own personal dearest version. You're a lucky superstar, Naydyr, well, we're both lucky, I guess!", joked Nero in the back of Naydyr's mind. Yes, Nero had been in synthesis with Naydyr even as far back as this, the year 2036.

And yes, Pei Piezhi was the reincarnation of Poppaea, the most prominent of all of Nero's numerous wives and lovers, and consequently, and with earnest honesty, his favorite, being his true soulmate. But she didn't know that yet, at this point in time. Like the rest of the human race, she would only be directly contacted by Poppaea herself after the Dead Man's Hand Detonation Event, in 2050. This was, rather painfully and even sadly, if you will, something that Naydyr knew to be true, that she could never resonate with him, in, say, the same way that Ruslan did.

Ruslan was also an attendant at the wedding, for he was with his own wife, Polina Taisaya. Polina was, rather interestingly, the reincarnation of the goddess Persephone. You must understand, for yes, it was true that the Greek gods were real, physical beings, but they were not "gods" in the sense that they were higher dimensional, transient, untouchable beings, but instead, they were very real, physical, primordial humans. The Greek gods were, in fact, just very ancient humans who possessed the strongest, rawest, and most original of genes in the human gene pool's history, and coupled with a significantly higher amount of oxygen in that ancient atmosphere, they were much larger, in size and stature. In addition, the incredibly powerful genetic makeup of these Greek gods was so in harmony with nature, that they were capable of what can only be described as "magic", or "sorcery", by today's standards. Think of Zeus's lightning bolts, or Poseidon's control over water. It was most upsetting, to the select few who were aware of this lost knowledge, that humans had then gone so long without honing and practicing these magical powers, that genetically, throughout the generations and millennia of genetic deterioration, coupled with the neglect of practice, these magic powers had become lost, as the descended human race was no longer connected to "nature" in the same way it had been, with "nature" really being a broad term for reality at large. And by genetic deterioration, I am referring specifically to the introduction of endocrine disrupting chemicals and harmful, genetic-altering substances, which have been poisoning humanity ever since the dawn of hyper-civilizing effort.

Persephone was one of the cleverest of these primordial humans, ruling and having power over that of the harvest, agriculture, and spring. Ruslan wed her not only because he loved her, respecting her highly, for being a Greek god or goddess in your past life was one of the most maximal honors within the occult, but also because of tactical reasons, for her personal happiness ensured bountiful food supplies for the P.S.E.

"Polina, my dearest, how are you feeling? What an incredible celebration of life, and love", inquired Ruslan to his wife.

Ruslan, who was, as described before, much less talkative and more stoic usually, was always liveliest around Polina, for she was the calming, welcoming fire to his cool, tempered ice, bringing him out of his shell, always encouraging him to express himself. It is also worth mentioning that Rasputin himself never really had a proper lover, in his time all the way back then, and so with Ruslan being lucky enough to wed a Greek goddess, Rasputin reminded him constantly of how fortunate he was. To Ruslan himself, he acknowledged this, and felt that his solace and loneliness as Rasputin must've been the necessary penance, the required unfulfillment, for him to then be rewarded so graciously with Polina's presence in his life, with Persephone, what a wonderfully impressive catch.

"I am so glad I married someone with great influence, like you Ruslan, I never had any lover before who would be able to take me to such an important event, let alone get us such exclusive seats... But oh, Ruslan, look! I think it's time for Sesto Latif to perform!", Polina said excitedly as her disposition went from grateful, to feverishly ecstatic.

It was then that the slow, romantic music had died down, and Sesto himself had taken control of the lead microphone, announcing, "Ladies and gentleman, let us please give a round of applause for our empire's most blessed and most benevolent Great Leader, Naydyr Chanming, and our empire's First Lady of the Revolution, the newly wed, Pei Chanming!"

He knew how to play to the crowd, and read the room.

And this ushered in a terrifically thunderous applause, which was also met with callouts, screams, and chants, displaying the fervently supercharged idolization these, most truthfully described as subjects to a higher power, felt for their leader and his wife. It was then that Sesto made his way onto the main center of the, again, ginormous, reception hall, where he was to perform for Naydyr, Pei, and the rest of everyone there.

Sesto Latif was a French musical artist and performer, commonly understood internationally to rank just second behind the iconic Pei in fame, in the charts, and in the number of fans. But because of Pei's considerable fake followers and fake online support, both Naydyr and Pei together knew him to be the true, actual number one artist in the world. They respected him greatly, for this. Sesto, unlike Pei however, was not a pop artist, but more of an underground hip-hop artist, although he wasn't exactly "underground" anymore, and hadn't been for years. He was, though notably, still loyal to his roots, and his music was markedly unique and different from anyone else. It was characterized by floaty, dreamy, cloudy beats, with nihilistic, dark, but spellcasting lyrics. He was a favorite of Naydyr's, and on his special day he would not have it any other way than to have a personal performance by Sesto himself, deep in the heart of the P.S.E.

Naydyr, in this year 2036, was 37 years old. Sesto had only been born himself in 2014, making him only 22 years old at that time.

Sesto was quite the young trailblazer.

So yes, Naydyr was quite the "hip" older gentleman! Personalized nanomachine technology had indeed already been implemented inside him, rendering him the deliberately chosen appearance of a 25-year-old, but none-the-less, he was very much invested in the modern music scene. Having had a taste for Hip-Hop at such a refined age, this was yet another dimension to his character that made him so likable and relatable to many young people around the world, and those especially in the Western democratic world. Perhaps it was not as surprising to some, for Naydyr was born in 1999, and would've been around 20 years old by the time Hip-Hop dominated the world's charts, in the 2010's and into the 2020's. By this year, 2036, it was apparent that Hip-Hop and C-Pop were the two largest genres of music in the world, primarily credited to the sheer dominance of both Pei and Sesto, respectively.

As Naydyr and Pei wrapped up their intimate slow-dance session, Naydyr then gestured for his guests to then join him on the dance floor, for it was about to get "lit", or really "turned up", as those who grew up in his generation would appropriately say.

Sesto, then gripping the microphone, and with the foggy, hazy, pounding, jaded crescendos and rhythmic melodies of his most famous song, "Clout By Jest", Sesto began to rap his song, live. Everybody in the colossal reception area danced to this song, and there was of course alcohol involved, to even more so enhance the festive mood. Everyone was happy. Naydyr, Pei, and even Ruslan and Polina, were all having the times of their lives, dancing and grooving to Sesto's rapping, and the beautiful instrumental of the song. For Sesto, perhaps in the easiest way to describe his musical direction, was not an aggressive rapper, nor a braggadocious rapper, but more of a smooth rapper. He glided on the beat, he levitated on top of the track, like a gust of mist floating from one end of the room to another. Sesto, quite impressively, was a one-of-a-kind musical artist, and Naydyr, someone who was a failed artist in his past life, knew good art when he saw it, and henceforth he adored and appreciated Sesto's creation of original, admirable, unique art.

Ruslan, dancing with Polina, said to her, quite drunkenly, "This Sesto Latif guy is so talented!"

It was truly, in every sense of the word, a good ole' fashioned Soviet communist party!

Everyone was having a great time!

Polina, equally as drunk, replied "I know! Surely us people of the P.S.E. know opulence and art better than anyone else!"

Polina, having been Persephone, held a natural elitist streak to her, not necessarily dominating her character, but to those who knew her, knew it was part of her true essence. For Persephone had been a Greek goddess after all, one who had looked down at the "mortals".

Sesto would go on to perform many more of his hit songs, and as the wondrous night came to a close, he lamented to himself, for it was indeed one of his first times ever entering the P.S.E. The nation of France, in which Sesto was native to, had purposely aligned itself against the P.S.E. in being a prominent upholder of democracy, a member of the U.N., as well as being a close ally of N.A.T.O. However, France and the P.S.E. still held suitable enough foreign relations, as World War III had not officially begun yet, not until 2039, which was an entire three years away.

After many hours into the late night, a night of lovely drinking, joking, conversing, and dancing, Naydyr had then found a moment to speak with Sesto personally, as Sesto had finished performing and was enjoying himself a White Russian cocktail, the finest edition of one anyone could find on earth. Naydyr, smiling at Sesto, walked over slowly, for he was not without his own consumption of wine and drinks himself. This was his true character after all, as Nero had been known to be a glutton addicted to wine himself.

"That man preformed an incredible act tonight,

Naydyr. You ought to thank him heavily for it, he made both myself and your dearest Pei very amazed and pleased this very special night!", hollered Nero to Naydyr, for Nero had been a would-be musical performer himself, as well, that was, when he was neglectfully ignoring his duties as emperor. He appreciated and held such an advanced taste of art and music, having been a consciousness over 2000 years old, that he knew great art when he saw it.

Naydyr made intense eye contact with Sesto then, and Sesto felt like Naydyr was staring into his very soul. Naydyr held a gaze of incredible focus, perhaps contrasted with the absolutely horrid condition of eyebags and dark circles under them. But to Naydyr, these eyebags and dark circles were his beauty statement, and in P.S.E. propaganda, they were evidence of the Great Leader who worked so tirelessly for his people, sacrificing many sleepless nights in the name of their well-being and quality of life. This was half true. A vast portion of the severity of Naydyr's eye appearance was because he was sleeplessly consuming stimulant-class drugs to then raise his consciousness, to then communicate with literal demons, through looking at and interfacing with an enchanted crystal ball.

He was an occult freak.

But alas, Naydyr and Sesto were face-to-face.

"An incredible performance tonight, for all of us! Tell me, my dearest guest, how have you enjoyed your time in my empire, the People's Soviet Empire? Be honest, your opinion means so very much to me", Naydyr said with a penetrating, laser-beam like, inquisitorial tone, which was more like an order, almost.

Because when Naydyr interacted with people who were not Presidents, or High Chancellors, or Prime Ministers, be it the regular man or woman, he easily overpowered them with his presence. Naydyr was someone who had, in the most remarkable of terms, conjoined the two historically separate nations of Russia and China together, through masterful diplomacy and negotiation, as well as having resurrected both the spirit and namesake of the Soviet Union. So, in having a casual conversation with someone who was more of a civilian, Naydyr had mastered social and human interaction.

He was comparable to a serpent.

Sesto, then, looking down to gain some more confidence, for he knew exactly who he was speaking to, then looked back into Naydyr's anticipatory eyes, and said, "Quite frankly, it's been maybe the most eye-opening and wonderful experience of my life. You are such an impressive individual, sir, you truly have changed the world and created a land unlike any other. Your power and influence are immeasurable, truly, it has been an honor to even be invited to your wedding at all, let alone preform, Great Leader."

He wanted to make a good impression.

Sesto had spent just six days so far in the P.S.E., and in an effort unbeknownst to him, not unlike North Korea's fake tourist destinations and hotels intended to impress outsiders, Sesto was carefully and precisely presented with the most illustrious and impressive places, areas, and locations the P.S.E. had to offer. The poverty-stricken areas, the communistic block towers, gulags, labor camps, and the such, were of course, veiled away. Many people suffered tremendously in the P.S.E., do not be mistaken, for it was, after all, a "Soviet Union 2.0", as some American economists labeled it.

Naydyr smiled. For his smile... was a devilish smile.

"Quite the flattery! I like this young man tremendously, he knows respect. When respect is given, respect is deserved. Naydyr, I think he's earned the right to know... who he really is. Tell him you'd like to invite him to one of our inner-meetings, with the good ole' boys, you know. Tell him you'll go on your honeymoon with Poppaea and then you'd like to have him back, in about 2 months. There, we will see if he's game or not. If he's a real deal player", Nero instructed Naydyr, all the while that Naydyr and Sesto took a brief pause in their conversation, where they both observed the lights and jovialness of the afterparty, which was coming to a close.

"I'd like to have you back, here, in my homeland, in about two months. I'll go on my honeymoon with my wife, who loved your performances by the way, and in the meantime, as you're escorted back home to France, one of my comrades will give you my phone number. Thank you so much, truly, from the depths of my being... I'll be in touch!", Naydyr then winked and smiled, completely and utterly flabbergasting Sesto.

You see, you must not forget, for no matter how popular internationally Sesto was and knew himself to be, Naydyr was still the most powerful and influential, and arguably important man on planet earth. The richest, the most controversial, the most talked about, everything, for by 2036, Naydyr was in the prime of his leadership.

Sesto, attempting to contain himself and regain his composure, looked up at Naydyr, and squeaked out a "Thank you, the honor was all mine, congratulations again!"

Naydyr then shook his hand, and turned around, to walk back to Pei, not before rotating slightly, halfway, and then uttering a single phrase.

"Adieu, Sesto."

Sesto smiled back, and waved. His short confrontation with the devil's representation on earth had been brief, but physically drained him of immense energy, for it was almost as if, he suspected, or floated the idea in his mind, that their handshake had siphoned some life-force from him. He brushed it off, thinking he must've just been fatigued from his performances.

"Cupid", Nero said slyly.

"He's Cupid, Naydyr."

CHAPTER 4

Proclamation for the Ages

May 5th, 2030, 1:50 P.M.

White House Confidential Meeting Room,
Washington D.C., The United States of America

"This is… bad", offered up Alaric Georgi.

"Wow", said Henry Cursor.

Henry, the Vice President, who was Hercules in his past life, was awakening his warrior spirit, his war-hawk essence, for his wisdom and intelligence allowed him to foresee an unavoidable conflict, given what had just transpired. However, in only what the truest of warriors and fighters would understand, Henry was also concerningly rejecting this impulse, for it meant the spilling of his people's blood, the shattering of families, and the erasure of innocence, and peace, and joy. In this very moment, he was impressing Hercules very much, for Hercules could feel his concern for his American people, a genuine trademark of a proper hero, while all the while becoming ready for battle, a most quintessential aspect of a noble, admirable leader.

Do not be mistaken, though, for Henry had no synthesis with Hercules's consciousness yet, none of the Americans had. Only Naydyr and Ruslan possessed this advantage at this point in time.

"Surely, there will be a war", mused Henry.

"It's inevitable", reasoned Alaric.

Alaric, the 51st President of the United States, and starting this very day, the foremost voice and preeminent leading figure on how to approach what had just happened, and what it meant for the free world, the democratic world, and the very direction of human history, was thinking and musing heavily, what angle he should take, in his State of the Union address later that night.

For it was a rather terrifying, worrying, scary time for the entirety of the Western, and democratic world. There was a singular man on almost every screen and news channel in the world at that particular hour, speaking in a fiery, monstrous, emotionally unstable, rabid, manic, possessed manner. This man was a 31-year-old, who had been known previously only as a crafty businessman and savvy negotiator, a political essayist and economic-theory novelist, as well as even an influential spiritualist, in recent years.

I really wonder who this could be…

Oh, that's right, it's obvious.

The one and only, newly crowned and ordained Soviet Emperor, Naydyr Chanming, now First Citizen of the People's Soviet Empire, the literal King of Death on earth.

Anyways, he was, on this particular day, most satanically energized, and his announcement speech, which also doubled as an inauguration ceremony, as well as a hidden-in-plain-sight satanic anointing, was a proclamation for the ages. It consisted of bold statements, other-worldly assumptions, broad and sweeping conclusions, and even references to the scripture.

"And on this very day, May 5th, in the year 2030, the start of a new, yet to be spoiled, decade, may all workers and laborers of the world unite and rejoice! For it is on this very day, May 5th, that we celebrate the birthday of the great, extensively-gifted, and wondrous visionary that was the talented thinker, Karl Marx!", Naydyr roared with a fiery aggression, swinging his fists up and down, forcibly rocking his head back and forth when he spoke, and gripping his pedestal as if he was about to throw it, or destroy it.

"Well, he is quite the actor, indeed", Henry offered as his commentary, as both him and Alaric watched their television screen, previewing the news. Every news channel on the face of the earth was covering this speech. People in Europe, India, Australia, and all over, were in their homes, peeking into stores, tuning in on their smartphones, for this was the most viewed single broadcast in modern industrialized human history. Of the then roughly 10 billion people on earth at the time, approximately 7 billion were watching.

Henry was also unimpressed, largely. He was unintimidated by Naydyr. He didn't really respect him, although he had heard of him before this, for in seeing his true character, he thought of him as a charlatan, a serpent, a snake oil salesman, a degenerate. He knew with utmost certainty he would lead his people to destruction. In fact, he thought of him as a loser.

Truthfully, was Naydyr a loser?

Maybe.

Probably.

"For listen closely, and listen well, any that may lend their ear to my voice, for in this current age of the hyper-civilized, ultra-exploited, fatally-capitalistic world in which so many countless souls yearn for something greater, having felled prey to the grasps of an ever-encompassing selfishness, a stain on the human essence, may you feel liberated, may you raise your arms and lift your fist in pride, and glory!", Naydyr proclaimed in an eruption of triumphant, victorious righteousness.

He continued, almost building momentum as he proceeded to astound the entire world, with his pure vehemence, his seemingly monstrous dictation, stating, "Marx, may you look down at us all, the ones in which you so predictively wrote for in the sake of us, may you smile, for a new and powerful communist state shall materialize before your very eyes, our prophet Marx, for the misunderstood and besmirched Soviet Union shall be resurrected, and our strong and impressive communist China, a beacon of the validity of your ideals and an inspiring testament to your eternal genius, shall join this second Soviet Union! On your very birthday, the 212th anniversary of your ordained entry to our history books, may you smile, for the historic nations of Russia and China have come together, in a unification of all ages, something that has never happened before!"

Naydyr was in his absolute prime in this very speech. No one could fathom, those unsuspecting of the news, how this man had just managed to then in what seemingly what felt like an instant, ascertain complete and utter control of what was now an empire rivaling even that of the antiquated British Empire or even the Mongolian Empire of the Khans.

Life had just gotten "very real" for many, many people.

"Stupid idiot doesn't get that communism is played out", Henry stung quickly, conveying absolutely no respect for what he had just heard and seen, dismissing it entirely.

"His belly is fatter than his brain, that is for sure", Alaric layered onto the barrage of verbal assaults.

In another conversation happening unbeknownst to both Alaric and Henry, in their very same room and presence, was one between Alexander the Great and Hercules, for past life consciousnesses were permanently clung to their second, new, current life, physical vessels, being Alaric and Henry, and in the absence of dialogue with them, they were still able to, for each being in the spirit world, able to recognize each other, and converse with each other.

They talked to each other immensely, well, because they couldn't talk to Alaric or Henry, not yet, not until the Dead Man's Hand Detonation Event of December 9, 2050. And this was a stark contrast to the differing case of Nero and Rasputin, who seldom talked to each other because they were busy conversing with their own current life vessels, Naydyr and Ruslan. Albeit, they did sometimes exchange minor banter, but primarily, they were occupied instructing and advising their own physical, secondary incarnations.

As Naydyr became more and more demonically possessed, Henry couldn't help but continue his tirade of disrespect, further berating him by saying "What an ugly man, he has such a fat neck. He reminds me of someone like Nero Caesar, from Roman history. Just a rabid, uncontrolled, moronic megalomaniac."

"Very funny, Hercules. Your little project pinned the nail on the head, perhaps that's the true eagle eye of a tactician of your caliber? He recognizes that Naydyr is similar to Nero, but doesn't realize yet that he quite literally is... Nero! Oh, the irony of the gods! Homer would've loved this prime banter", Alexander the Great couldn't help by erupt in laughter to himself, as he and Hercules watched and listened to their two students, sons, soldiers, pupils, all of the sort wrapped in one, for they did, in fact, love these two strong men very much, having been with them their whole lives, watching them, and protecting them, all from their hidden veil in the spirit world. Alexander the Great and Hercules, were in fact, two men who could relate to and respect each other very much, being perhaps two of some of the most legendary figures in all of Western civilization. It made sense, as well, that Alexander would be the President, and Hercules his Vice President, for Hercules, despite being already impressive enough as a soldier and leader, was not the conqueror and statesman that Alexander was. In the same respect that Nero and Rasputin found commonality in their wickedness, Alexander the Great and Hercules found kinship in their righteous justice.

"My little Henry is thirsting for some blood, this coming war will be his opportunity to prove himself to me, he's been itching for something like this his whole life, whether he's just realizing it or not", Hercules replied to Alexander the Great. Henry was in fact, a former military captain and promoted five-star general. Before that, he was a professional baseball player, a designated hitter, who had his own legendary career, being a multiple-time champion. This of course bolstered his popularity when he transitioned to a politician, endearing himself to the locals, the children, and the regular people of the nation. He was the ultimate figure of masculinity, fittingly so, as Hercules's new and improved vessel, with a dominating presence, and yet, he was equally blessed in intelligence, an erudite, having often spent time writing poetry, and practicing the acoustic guitar. Henry was, by all accounts, a man worthy of being President, and he knew in due time he probably would eventually, one day, run for election again and then fulfill yet another chapter of his illustrious, legendary life. However, in this shocking and foreboding news of Naydyr's ascension to demonic power, he wondered if the United States would ever see another stable enough decade for him to be elected, after Alaric's second term ended. For he wondered to himself, much to Hercules's delight, whether his ultimate destiny was maybe not to be the greatest Vice President, and later President, but rather a re-entry to his military days, perhaps his ultimate destiny was to lead the military forces of the United States in swift and effective leadership, having defeated this new communist enemy, a threat to America of all ages. Yes, Henry reasoned to himself, his ultimate destiny lies not in any skilled diplomacy as a political leader, or as a future President, no, it lied in the battlefield, harkening back to the best days of his life, as a military captain and later general. The brotherhood and camaraderie he had with his soldiers was Henry's edition of Hercules's bond with his own fellow warriors. Henry no longer envisioned himself as any future President, no, he knew his true purpose in life layed on the battlefield, directing his fellow warriors.

He had, in truth, already surpassed the legacy of some of the greatest American generals, but he lacked the necessary conflict many of these generals served under, being World War II, to test and measure his own capabilities as a warrior king.

Hercules was proud of Henry, he was proud... for Hercules, after all, was remembered in history more for being a warrior, having slain the Nemean Lion with his bare hands, than he was for politics.

Henry stared at Alaric, and sincerely announced, as a promise rather than a statement, that "I will defeat this new enemy swiftly and with the vengeance of our forefathers. I have waited for a conflict like this one which is predictably coming, to demonstrate my abilities to you."

Alaric cracked a smirk, and chimed back, "Is the famed Henry the Destroyer making a comeback to the battlefield, it seems so? Your mech suit hasn't seen the light of day for a while now."

Henry, fittingly appropriate for being Hercules's second coming, held a personal kill-count of around 3,000, hand-slain that is. Don't forget, this was the era of cyber-ninjas, and super soldier death machines.

"Nothing pleases me more than the spilling of a demon's blood", Henry said sternly, this was serious.

Alexander the Great let out a burst of laughter, "Hercules my brother, you're Henry is scaring my little Alaric!"

Hercules, in a somber tone, replied "That Nero is our greatest threat."

And Alaric and Henry knew who their rival was, now.

The sides of the chess board had been set.

The greatest, ultimate conflict between the West and East was now primed to go.

Who would really last, though, through it all?

CHAPTER 5

History Lesson

September 15^h, 2036, 3:00 A.M.

Gatchina Palace, Gatchina, Russia,
The People's Soviet Empire

It had been around two months since Sesto and Naydyr spoke, with Sesto and Naydyr having bid farewell to each other, agreeing upon a reuniting with each other, after Naydyr's honeymoon with Pei. They had texted sparsely, but Naydyr's text messages quite honestly consisted predominantly only of his expressed desire to have Sesto back, under his hospitality, he had not explained to them what it is they would do, once Sesto would return. They had, in total, over the course of the two months or so, exchanged maybe ten or so messages, only. Sesto, at the request and summoning of Naydyr's personal agents, had returned to the P.S.E., where very quickly and immediately, he knew this go around wasn't exactly the same innocent, normal, or familiar type of vibe as his time at the wedding. Naydyr had Sesto escorted to Gatchina Palace, which had been constructed in the 1770's in the region of Gatchina, just 28 miles south of St. Petersburg. The Gatchina Palace itself was monumentally overwhelming in size and breadth, and Sesto was driven in perhaps the nicest automobile he had ever been in; a beautiful luxury vehicle, which was the nicest car he had ever seen. Sesto then, if he hadn't already been in awe over the size and magnitude of the castle, had just realized he then had to prepare himself mentally and socially for engaging with Naydyr again, who he still felt drained him of energy when they interacted. Sesto's ride pulled through the castle gates, and Sesto could see the security which was present, being heavily armed, heavily armored, P.S.E. cyber-ninjas. He was a little afraid.

The luxury vehicle parked itself just before the impressive stairs of the entrance to the castle manor, and Sesto's door was opened for him, by a very rigid, stern chauffeur. He stepped out of the vehicle, and it occurred to him that the exact nature of his revisitation to the P.S.E. wasn't exactly specified in what regards it would entail. He had agreed to come back, but he had then realized that Naydyr himself, in his hypnotizing charm, had omitted what the two of them would be doing. If Sesto could remember, all he recalled was that Naydyr had said he "wanted him back in his homeland", leaving out any further details of what that precisely meant.

Sesto then received a text, it was from Naydyr. It read, "Coming out now, friend."

Naydyr then emerged from this particular entrance of the castle, and he was accompanied by Ruslan. Ruslan and Sesto were, in total honesty, only somewhat acquainted, for Ruslan wasn't very talkative to what he perceived as "outsiders", nor was he artistic in any regard, so there wasn't the same connection, the same dialogue, for Ruslan and Sesto as there was with Naydyr and Sesto. Regardless, Naydyr had a very emotive, distinctly visible from afar, smile that was beaming up his entire presence. Sesto processed up the stairs leading to the gigantic door frame, which looked to have been intended for literal giants to have walked through, and he stood just meters away from Naydyr, who was still smiling, almost unsettlingly so. Ruslan sized up Sesto, looking him up and down, and then held out his hand, for a handshake.

Ruslan locked his murky, aged, gray eyes with Sesto's young, seemingly feeble, and intimidated, brown eyes, and together they connected on a handshake.

"I believe we had spoken briefly, at the wedding, but allow me to properly introduce myself, for I am Ruslan Payurov, Highest Grand Chancellor of the People's Soviet Empire, and the second-in-command and second-highest authority, in this land. It is my pleasure to spend this evening with you, Sesto. You are a very impressive young man, we admire you greatly", spoke Ruslan with a commanding, yet welcoming tone, which eased Sesto's nerves slightly, but also woke him up from the tiredness of his long journey.

You must not forget; Sesto had traveled all alone.

He was increasingly aware of this as the moment progressed to the next moment.

"I, uh, am very honored, Ruslan. It's nice to meet you, truly", Sesto squeaked under his breath. Ruslan was also 6'7" tall, while Sesto was, in comparison, 5'10" tall. Rasputin was noted for his large statue, and thus so was Ruslan. His hand dwarfed Sesto's as well.

Naydyr, still smiling, then shook Sesto's hand as well, and gestured for the trio of them to then enter the castle. As Sesto walked through the castle, he couldn't help but notice the décor of the building, and the almost unfathomably high ceilings, and foreboding, alternate paths leading wherever in God's name they led. Sesto reasoned to himself, of course, there must be a dungeon or two in this castle. But as he and Naydyr caught up, in Naydyr asking him how his trip was, and the such, he felt more comfortable, and at ease. The bodyguards and cyber-ninjas were also no longer with them, having been dismissed by Naydyr with the gesture of a finger twirl, and Naydyr explained to Sesto that he would like to lead him to what he called, the "Members Only Room".

Sesto was becoming increasingly confused, and was even floating the idea in his head if he had just willingly, and foolishly, surrendered himself to become a political prisoner, in an effort to extort France, or if he was about to be sacrificed to demonic gods, his mind was racing wildly.

It was in this moment of exasperation, that Sesto must've been too obviously disturbed, for Ruslan, who was following from slightly behind, then put his hand on Sesto's left shoulder, and said "You're sweating, relax, friend. Maybe this will ease your insurrectional spirit", and with one single tap of two fingers on the back of the neck, Sesto was knocked unconscious, and crumpled to the floor, from where he fell like a ragdoll.

It was then that Naydyr's smile metamorphosed into an eruption of insanely, unboundedly, unstable like crackling, a laughter indicative of a truly evil, disturbed person.

"I always love when you do that! It's funnier every time!", Naydyr exclaimed.

"That's that Russian eastern mysticism, that dark, occult, esoteric magic. I must say, Naydyr, you superstar, that it tickles me seeing that Rasputin had subdued the Romanovs in this very castle over a century ago, in the same way, and here is Ruslan doing the exact same thing, I swear all of life's a play! Incessant little bodies, they all are, puny little pawns of unimportant destinies!", Nero proclaimed in his own short, equally disturbed soliloquy, clamoring to what he perceived as art before his very eyes, being the "play" that was all of life.

"Shush, I actually really like this fellow right here, I'm hoping he'll decide to be a player, and won't fumble", Naydyr uttered back.

Fast forward about an hour, and it was 3 A.M., the "devil's hour". Sesto opened his eyes, and he was in a giant circular room, with a giant statue of a Roman emperor, he could deduce, that looked amazingly spotless, and new, as if it wasn't an ancient relic, but rather a recreated replica, a modern piece of art.

Sesto was not chained, or shackled, or tied up, or

anything of the sort. He did have the retained memory of being forcibly sent into unconsciousness, but he did not feel sore, in the body or mind, nor did he feel threatened, or that his life was in danger. He was, actually, seated in a very comfortable chair, that he felt his body was sinking into, devouring him, being so comfortable and soft that he did not want to deny himself the pleasure of sitting in it, he didn't feel any impulse to run away for his life. In front of him was Naydyr, and Ruslan, sitting in their own chairs, patiently staring at him, as if they had been studying him while he loaded back into an awake state. He stared back at them, but he was speechless, he didn't know what to say. Naydyr, even still, had a devious smile, as if he was so unabashedly delighted.

"Now, Sesto, if there is anything I love more than myself, and my wife, and my empire I have created for myself, then it is probably the act of talking! Yes, I love to talk, I love to give long, lengthy speeches, I love to explain things, to teach, and illuminate, I love sharing my knowledge with others, those who are ready for... it", Naydyr quickly said with an incessant aura of enthusiasm.

Naydyr continued his speech, saying in an endearing, although slightly patronizing, tone, saying, "Sesto, my dear friend, my fine young man, I just want you to know that we don't intend to harm you, no, we only aim to help you. Ruslan and I figured it would simply be best if you just woke up... in this room here, rather than take the trip awake! There were some... unavoidable spectacles along the path that... I think it was best we spared you from seeing."

Now what exact atrocities, monstrosities,

unforgettable, trauma-inducing visuals and instances was Naydyr alluding to, or was the foreboding description of these things an exaggeration, a lie? No, the truth was this, that there were literal demons roaming the castle, having been summoned in deeply primordial, ancient occult rituals. For this ever-expansive castle was the occult-castle, where dark exercises.... were performed. If Sesto were to see one, surely, he would have a heart attack from the sheer fear. There was no use of Sesto if he was dead.

Sesto then pursed his lips to speak, to reply to Naydyr, but he couldn't, he couldn't speak, no matter what, he had lost his ability to formulate and pronounce syllables, to conjoin together words and say them, he was mute.

Ruslan, having been focusing on Sesto like a hawk, then explained to him, "Sesto, let me first apologize for subduing you, it was just a harmless trick, really, I simply channeled the energy from my uncalcified pineal gland into my fingertips, projecting my heart's intent and focusing my manifested energies, into a visualized ball of light, which I then extended into you, through our physical contact. And with your body, and by extension, light-body, being largely unshaped, unfocused, and vulnerable to spiritual attacks, my focused energy simply overpowered you instantly, and rendered you unconscious. It's a fickle thing, really, to have developed these powers, and then to remember that nobody else could even conceive of them."

Rasputin laughed in the back of Ruslan's mind, bellowing how, "In my day, I could accomplish the same effect through mere eye contact."

Naydyr looked down, and smiled even more, for Sesto was beginning to understand, that these two men were very wicked men, they practiced dark arts, occult sciences, perverse alchemy, communication with demons, and spirits, and he didn't even put it past them to maybe have been leaders of sacrificial rituals. Sesto's eyes widened, but he could not get up from the chair. He looked away, in terror, but all he could lock his eyes on was the giant Roman statue, and he noticed how it resembled Naydyr. Naydyr would then go on to begin yet another one of his soliloquies.

"I want to teach you a lesson, today, Sesto. Class is in session!", Naydyr announced triumphantly, as he then was handed a book, a rather old, aged, antiquated book, in which he then opened up using a bookmark in between the pages.

Sesto, still heavily under the residual hypnosis of Ruslan's spiritual attack, accepted that he had no choice but to entertain this scary relaying of knowledge, whatever it was that they would want to teach him, he figured it was better than being executed. There were, of course, guns in the room, as well, off to the side.

"Do you believe in Destiny, Sesto, or do you believe in the naivety of Free-Will? For the two are irreconcilable, truthfully, for how can a person, as a human, have a fate that they actively fulfill, more and more, every day, and yet, they also have an unbridled freedom, this flimsy, loosely defined, 'Free-Will'? I think not, for allow me to prove it to you!", echoed Naydyr throughout the rooms and chambers of the castle.

Naydyr then officially began his lecture, joyously

talking in a singing tone, "Sesto, you are Christian, yes? As you hail from the historically faithful nation of France, well, allow me to read you, my wonderful and divinely chosen student, an excerpt from the Sibylline Oracles, a collection of Christian and Jewish apocalyptic verses, based on the prophecies of an ancient woman, Sibyl, who identified herself as a native of Babylon. It is also worth mentioning that she claimed to have been a daughter of Noah, of the flood, although historians now entertain the possibility that she may have been rather a daughter-in-law."

Ruslan cracked a slight chuckle to himself, as he and Rasputin were making fun of Naydyr, privately, in how, perhaps in another parallel, alternate dimension, or timeline, Naydyr was a harmless, obsessive teacher or professor, rather than a demon invoking dictator.

Sesto was listening intently. He had still felt devoured by the chair he was sitting in, and he still felt incapable of moving or getting up, for Ruslan's spellcasting was still at work. Sesto had no choice other than to listen.

Naydyr, reading this book, read aloud, "For in this ancient work, this prophesier claimed that, 'One who has fifty as an initial, the Hebrew letter 'N', will be a grievous commander, a terrible snake, breathing out grievous war... but even when he disappears, he will be destructive. Then he will return declaring himself equal to God', volume 28, my most attentive pupil!"

Sesto was beginning to understand what was happening, for Naydyr was... likening himself to the very figure that was being described in these ancient scriptures. It had never occurred to him that, maybe, Naydyr was so important he was, in actuality, a living, breathing, testament to the legitimacy of these ancient prophecies, in a world where many people did not even believe in God in the slightest. True and utter madness, he thought to himself, but he was beginning to see, to see what Naydyr had intended for him to learn that night.

"A very interesting excerpt, yes... for now let us continue our lesson tonight! For let us, Sesto, dive into the Christian poet Commodian, of the year A.D. 260, who also wrote, that 'Then, doubtless, the world shall be finished when he shall appear. He himself shall divide the globe into three ruling powers, when, moreover, Nero shall be raised up from hell, Elias shall first come to seal the beloved ones; at which things the region of Africa and the northern nation, the whole earth on all sides, for seven years shall tremble. But Elias shall occupy the half of the time, Nero shall occupy half. Then the harlot of Babylon, being reduced to ashes, its embers shall thence advance to Jerusalem; and the Latin conqueror shall then say, I am Christ, whom ye always pray to; and, indeed, the original ones who were deceived combine to praise him. He does many wonders, since his is the false prophet', reads the section 'Instructions', chapter 41, are you paying attention, Sesto?"

Sesto could not fathom the madness. His eyes were darting all over the place, he was looking for any semblance of sanity, for the man in front of him was the devil's representation on earth, the very figure these ancient texts were speaking of!

Naydyr then grabbed another book, a very aged, rustic looking book, and read some more, saying, "Sesto, allow me to read you just two more passages, yes? Can you handle that, are you getting the picture, now, Sesto?"

Ruslan tipped back his head, for he had heard these passages seemingly a million times, he scoffed, for he doubted that Sesto would join them, he doubted that he would understand in the way Naydyr so desperately had hoped for.

Naydyr continued, reading, "Allow me to read from the Testament of Hezekiah, where the prophet Isaiah wrote most fittingly, and accurately, that 'And after the world has been brought to completion, Beliar will descend, the great angel, the king of this world, which he has ruled ever since it existed. He will descend from his firmament in the form of a man, a king of iniquity, a murderer of his mother – this is the king of the world – and will persecute the plant which the twelve apostles of the Beloved will have planted; some of the twelve will be given into his hand. This angel, Beliar, will come in the form of that king, and with him will come all the powers of this world; he will act and speak like the Beloved, and will say, 'I am the Lord, and before me there was no one.' And all men in the world will believe in him', Chapter four, verses one through eight!"

Sesto, at this point, accepted the situation he was in. He realized, not unlike a quote he had heard long ago, that when you cannot change the situation or environment you are in, you must not fret, or fold, for you can still control how you react, and in that reaction lies the true condition of your being, not in what is around you, not in what could be in front of you. Sesto was no longer scared, rather, he understood, understood what Naydyr was attempting to do, which in a way, Sesto could appreciate, he appreciated that he was coming clean, revealing who he really was, revealing his true nature. In this moment, he decided to really listen to Naydyr's "lessons", he wanted to pick up on the details, to tell him more about Naydyr, who he was really dealing with.

"It doesn't look like he's panicked anymore, he's come to grips with what is going on, here", Ruslan offered up as his observation.

"Yes... yes, Sesto, you seem to have buckled down and now you're really absorbing my lesson! Nothing brings more delight to a teacher than to have his dearest pupils reciprocate his same energy, surely the greatest teachers of history, Socrates, Aristotle, surely, they look down at us now and send their very best blessings!"

Naydyr was incredibly energized as of right now, after all, he did say he loved to talk. Ruslan, however, having checked the time, was ready to move onto their other plans for the night, being the "ride out".

Ruslan brought this to Naydyr's attention, saying to him, "Naydyr, it's already 3:26, it'll be morning soon. Read him just one more passage, a short one. I think by looking at his expression, he knows by now."

Naydyr looked down, as if disappointed, but then he looked again at Sesto, and smiled. He then swapped books yet again, this time picking up a different book, and he began to read, "Alas, Sesto, may we end our little session on this final note, for allow us to dive into the writings of Irenaeus, a Greek bishop born in 130 A.D., who wrote 'Against Heresies', a collection of his takes on the Christian faith and its future. Irenaeus wrote here, that 'The name of the Beast possesses the number six hundred and sixty-six, since he sums up in his own person all the commixture of wickedness which took place previous to the deluge... and also sums up every error of devised idols since the flood, which shall come in the six hundredth year of Noah', volume 29, verse 2. And with that, my dearest student, our lesson has concluded. You are all dismissed!"

Naydyr, looking at Ruslan, then put this last book away, and looked at Sesto, curious if he could have grasped the magnitude of truth that he just had shared with him, but also disappointingly expectant, for he didn't reach Naydyr's personal hopes of appearing rejoiceful, so he already was not as enthusiastic as Naydyr would've hoped. That is, if one would be enthusiastic. He then said, "Sesto, it's time to roll out. Ruslan, give him control over his vessel now."

Ruslan then walked behind Sesto, and poked with his two fingers the back of Sesto's neck, and Sesto could talk again, and move, and he rose up out of the chair, and looked at Ruslan, and then looked at Naydyr.

Naydyr and Sesto locked eyes, and then Sesto, speaking for the first time in about an hour, said, "What do you mean by 'roll out', Naydyr?", with a blank expression, projecting true neutrality over what had just transpired.

And just like that, they were inside a topless, military grade vehicle, a monstrous automotive beast. This vehicle was a combination of a giant military-grade jeep while also having the size of a whole tank. But it ran on only four wheels. It was Naydyr, Ruslan, Sesto, and then two others, who were perceivable as another pair of Naydyr's two personal accomplices. All of them had Russian-styled, Russian-model assault rifles. These other two mysterious men were wearing a camouflage-styled turban-like scarf, as well as dark glasses. Sesto wondered why they were wearing them, when it was currently still 3 A.M., it was still very dark outside. Naydyr then said to one of these bodyguards, "Dagon, you ready to roll the camera? Okay, Dex, play the music. Everyone, get in your element."

Sesto noticed how they were all wearing extremely expensive designer clothing, and once the music turned on, Dagon, the mysterious accomplice, then started recording, and it became apparent, that Naydyr was filming his own music video, on a topless beast of a vehicle, and as the music started blaring, all of them started shooting their guns up in the sky and out in the distance, completely haphazardly and dangerously. The two mysterious accomplices, Dagon and Dex, were the craziest and most frantic moving, and while not being able to see their faces, Sesto became terrified if they were even human or not. But alas, they all were shooting their Russian assault rifles, laughing, dancing to their music, and having the time of their lives, in the music video. That was, everyone except Sesto, who was completely and utterly overwhelmed and bewildered by the sheer bizarreness of what he had gotten himself into.

Naydyr howled to himself, "Way too up!", into the camera recording him and his squad, and Naydyr then sprayed his Russian assault rifle into the air, firing upwards, with just one hand controlling the gun, while he made gestures and motions with his other hand.

After they had finished filming, and their little joy

ride came to an end, Sesto was so exhausted, even more so with it being about 4 A.M. by then. The warthog-like military truck then rolled back to where it had picked them up, and all of them got out. Including Sesto. The two men who hid their faces then went to Naydyr and said something quickly to him, then scurried out and away in an almost inhuman way, as if they were human bodies possessed by either aliens or demons, or something. But Sesto was jaded. He realized, now, that this is really how the world operates at this level of power and fame, he reasoned, and with Naydyr being the elite of the elite, it made sense to him, he wasn't scared anymore. But immediately, once the faceless two, Naydyr, and Ruslan had composed themselves, Naydyr immediately went to Sesto, and shot out his voice at him, in which he had not said anything to Sesto in the last 40 or so minutes.

"Sesto, you're Cupid, you know? The city of love itself, Paris, France, well Cupid personifies that very much, you, you are the truest born son of France, the Cupid, of love, that is who you were in your past life, Sesto, my boy!"

It was in this moment, where Naydyr was staring at Sesto intensely, to gauge his reaction at what he had just said, that Naydyr felt a singular pulse in his own heartbeat, that shook him immensely, for just a second. This jolt to the system that Naydyr felt was accompanied with a mental image of the phrase, "You're doing well", flashed across the innards of his mind.

He brushed it off, thinking that maybe it was a pure random thought due to a rusting of his mastery of his inner-thinking thought-loops, or maybe it was Nero's doing.

But he wouldn't forget it. Maybe, it was a sign from Cupid himself to pat him on the back or send his regards for shocking Sesto so much, and maybe Sesto and Cupid had achieved synthesis of their consciousnesses? That was what he hoped it was, he couldn't think of anything else. Either way, Sesto looked right back at Naydyr, and said, "What? What are you talking about?", with a blank stare.

Nero then said into Naydyr's head, slightly creating a pause in his disappointment, saying, "He is Cupid, this is obvious. But he hasn't made contact with Cupid yet, even after all this, he's thick in the skull, sadly. I say erase his recent memory, and send him home. He wasn't capable of being One of the Four, after all. I know you are disappointed, but he's not ready, he wasn't destined for just that, yet, in this timeline. Wipe him."

Naydyr's true intentions, in all of this, was to include Sesto as One of the Four Horsemen of the Apocalypse, being the White Rider of Conquest, the Red Rider of War, the Black Rider of Famine, and the Pale Rider of Death. This of course, being the Four as described in the Book of Revelations, the final installment of any normal, typical version of the Bible, found anywhere.

Naydyr was the White Rider of Conquest, through his ownership over such a landmass, Ruslan was the Black Rider of Famine, through his marriage and manipulation of his wife Persephone's influence over the harvest, and the Red Rider of War and the Pale Rider of Death were yet to be chosen, at this point in time.

What was originally planned, was for Sesto to awaken to his past life as Cupid, his synthesis moment, and for him to be quickly briefed on what to do, how to follow Naydyr's plan, for Naydyr possessed the most powerful soul, Nero's, and thus, he overpowered all the lesser souls, and could instruct them how to in turn instruct their own vessel's thought patterns. Naydyr had hoped to make Sesto his Pale Rider of Death, an honorary title that would be formally given to him through suitable proof of being synthesized with Cupid, and through pledging his loyalty to the P.S.E., Naydyr, Ruslan, and their destiny. However, Sesto seemed simply exhausted, and nothing seemed to indicate in him he had any idea what any of them was talking about, he was simply delirious from the waves of stimuli.

"I see.... Ruslan, erase his most recent memory and have him transported back to France, plant inside him the memories of a pleasant, sight-seeing trip. He did not break through, so he cannot compromise any of the sensitive information or things he witnessed or what was explained to him. Do away with him, he failed the test, a shame", Naydyr said with disgust, for nothing was of a greater wasted expenditure of energy than for him to have so thoroughly read him the scripture, raised his adrenaline levels enough through the music video's filming, and then for him to reveal his very past life to his very face, and all for nothing. Naydyr felt overall very disappointed, and a cloud of darkness was immediately casted over everyone in a five square mile radius, unknowingly.

Sesto looked terrified for what he just heard, before Ruslan then stepped out from behind him, and knocked him out again, through a touch. Ruslan would then conduct the necessary rituals to erase his mind and recent memory and then replace it with a myriad of fake instances of sightseeing. It would work, and Sesto would never know what he knew, or failed to know, in that one trip back to the P.S.E.

Naydyr looked down, still gripping his Russian assault rifle.

"A shame, Sesto Latif the Black Rider of Death would've been such a wickedly awe-inspiring title or what, am I right?", Naydyr said to Nero, in his head, in the depths of his innermost seat of consciousness.

Nero replied to Naydyr, saying, "It would have certainly been of epic proportions, but don't be disappointed, for this means the true role fulfiller here is even of greater deservedness, in the eyes of the fortune-tellers, the prophets, the oracles. Let it be known that we look forward to finding the next candidate."

Naydyr then smiled.

"That was quite the history lesson though", Naydyr said to Nero.

It was all in vain, though, unfortunately, he had thought to himself.

"We really could've been the best of friends, ever, but you weren't ready for that, I was too much, it seems", Naydyr reflected, in a solace mood.

And Sesto was returned home, and he went on living his life, thinking only of what a wonderful time he had in the P.S.E., yet again.

CHAPTER 6

War

May 8th, 2044, 12:50 AM

Ukrainka Air Base, Belogorsk, Russia,
The People's Soviet Empire

"We'll be encountering some company, shortly, it looks like some others would like to join the party", Naydyr said to Ruslan in a cold, foreboding, and unemotional tone.

This was during the peak of World War III. Naydyr and Ruslan were the two most wanted after men in the world, and really in all of history, at large.

The golden enthusiasm and ambition that permeated the P.S.E. had turned into a fierce and powerful disdain for the rest of the world, who was fighting them. And this in large part was due to a trickling down of moods from its leaders, Naydyr and Ruslan.

Ruslan, looking over and smirking, then replied back, "Looks like we'll be joined by none other than Joan of Arc, Richard of Lionheart, and Lawrence of Arabia. Quite a group, I must admit."

This was the trio of the assassination party that was planning on infiltrating Ukrainka Air Base, one of the largest P.S.E. military bases. Word had traveled to American intelligence that Naydyr would be making an appearance at this base, and he would be accompanied by Ruslan as well. According to the American intelligence's sources and operatives, the two would be visiting with the purpose of previewing new technology that could potentially sway the trajectory of the war, with it being so importantly devastating and advanced. The three special operations soldiers sent out on this mission were Joy Adelyn, who was Joan of Arc reincarnated, Raven Leverette, who was Richard of the Lionheart reincarnated, and lastly, Lyric Abdiel, who was Lawrence of Arabia reincarnated. Of course, however, none of them knew this whatsoever, and Joy would've been the first to achieve synthesis, for the Dead Man's Hand Detonation Event would not occur until seven years later, in 2050. It was only 2044, at this point in time, and fighting between the P.S.E.'s joint Chinese and Russian forces versus that of the combined American, European, N.A.T.O. and U.N. forces was at its peak around the world, in different countries, it was a world-wide conflict.

Lyric, into his intercom, which was integrated in with his cyber-ninja suit, said officially, "Well, Joy, Raven, let's see what's cooking in good old Ukrainka tonight, shall we?"

Lyric was the leader of this three-person mission. Joy and Raven were his two young, star pupils on the art and mastery of cyber-ninja suit maneuverability and destructive capacity. This was in fact an entirely newly birthed area of martial arts, being the creation of "Respect Limit", it was known as, for it referred to the Respect Limit held by your mech suit's artificial intelligence to either restrain or push you, and either bend or hold back your desired actions. It was a respect that the mech's adaptive computer system would adjust to you personally, and through mastery of focused intent and physical conditioning, one could unlock higher levels of destruction and control in a cyber-ninja suit, where the difference between someone like Joy, a mastered Respect Limit prodigy, and a regular P.S.E. henchman, was night and day.

The three of them sat on the outskirts of the base, from an advantaged viewpoint. All three of them were to accomplish, or seek out to accomplish, three distinct goals. The first goal of their highly secret, highly classified, highly important mission was to kill Naydyr Chanming. This would end the war. The second goal was to kill Ruslan Payurov. This would be instrumental in crippling a post-Naydyr era P.S.E., because without either Naydyr's cult of personality or his second-in-command, the P.S.E. would then be doomed to implode from poor leadership. The third goal, which was in effect, the least important, but still surely notable, was to reveal and recover whatever advanced technology that was being developed and tested there, at Ukrainka Military Base, where they had been tipped off as being where Naydyr would touch down to see it and perhaps test it himself. This had been relayed to American Intelligence through a myriad of cyber-infiltrations as well as direct operatives out in the field. The three instruments of God's saving justice, being Joan of Arc, Richard the Lionheart, and Lawrence of Arabia, altogether, made this military endeavor one for the ages, one where all the gods and spirits watched with great anticipation. Joy Adelyn, the reincarnation of the 15th century peasant woman turned French heroine in the Hundred Years War between France and England, was eager to add even more to her legend in battle, another battle for Joy, with Joan's hidden and indirect guidance, that would train and prepare her for her confrontation with Naydyr, and Ruslan, two highly unpredictable and dangerous individuals. Raven Leverette, who was the 12th century Medieval English Warrior King, Richard of the Lionheart, who fought in the Crusades, was no slouch either, and through his cooperation with the French woman Joy, and as an English man in his past life, this proved to be part of the ultimate destiny of both Joan and Richard each to fulfill, with this part being the cooperation of France and England, nations once at war in a Hundred Years War, to join together in justice and mutual honor in the hope of smiting a shared opponent, the P.S.E., the ultimate enemy to both France and England in each of their own countries' histories. They were led by someone who you would be hard-pressed to find any wiser, any more astute, which was Lyric Abdiel, the reincarnation of Lawrence of Arabia, who was leading this assassination and recovery mission, just as the Lawrence of Arabia had led the Arab Revolts against the Turks in World War I, where now with

Lyric, he would be guiding his future self to summarily end World War III, this time not in a brazen uprising, but in a covert, exact, calculated mission of elimination, for God knew how to complement and challenge each of our legacies in ways to bring about all sides of ourselves, all aspects of our character.

And so Lyric, Joy, and Raven were all sneaking around from the outskirts, all the way into the main base's tower. It was in the tower that they planned to hack the main, all-encompassing, all-access-breaching, all-security-passing terminals used in the main military base's primary overview computers. With their instant-hack-scan technology, in the holographic reader of their cyber-ninja suit's visor, they could then analyze all information coming in and out of the base, and from there, get the drop on Naydyr's location, as well as the location of the coveted, highly dangerous technology being developed. And thus, they all sneaked into the command center, having stealthily killed many P.S.E. guards along the way.

Lyric, stating into his intercom while wiping his sonically-charged blade's blood-ridden edge, said to Joy, "Scan and hack the computers, Joy."

Joy then walked up and approached the main terminals and computers, in the top command room they had sneaked into, which was located at the highest floor of the command tower.

"I think our three little musketeers have played their little stealth game long enough, what do you think, my emperor?", snickered Nero in the back of Naydyr's mind.

Naydyr and Ruslan knew that Lyric, Joy, and Raven were there, at the base, because they could sense their soul essence, their energies drawing closer to their proximity, they could be informed of their presence as well from their own past life consciousnesses too, above all else, and it was on this hidden, spiritual battlefield that only Naydyr and Ruslan were operating on, which allowed them to always remain plenty of steps ahead of their enemies.

For Lyric, Joy, and Raven were all in complete honesty, unbeknownst to the fact that they could be tracked that way, or that their location could be determined that way, which only Naydyr and Ruslan were capable of.

All of Naydyr's and Ruslan's high commands and strategic decisions for managing the behemoth that was the People's Soviet Empire's economy, military, and all manners of affairs, were in fact always in large part decisions that were primarily advised, calculated, and ruminated upon by that of course being Nero and Rasputin, who both as separate, guiding consciousnesses for Naydyr and Ruslan to follow, were also closely feeding the two with information on all sorts of matters. This may have been economic trade matters, or strategic military emplacements and decisions, and all the topics of that nature.

It was an unfair advantage, most definitely, and Naydyr and Ruslan would be the only two to achieve this level of synthesized communication with their past life consciousness until the year of 2050, where the Dead Man's Hand Detonation Event would trigger the forcible connection with a majority of survivors, consequent from a forcible tear in the fabric of reality between the physical, apparent world and the invisible, spirit world. But none of that would transpire until 2050... not until December of that year, not until the ninth.

Naydyr, who was then sitting in a dark room, in one of the many hidden away rooms on the base's grounds, monitoring the three assassins every movement, then looked at Ruslan, with yearning eyes and a distanced expression, and held up two fingers, and twirled them slowly, in an alerting fashion, as to get the attention of a dog, or to even resume filming on a movie set. In reality, it was his way of signaling to Ruslan that things were about to get intense, so ready yourself, and also to communicate through a symbol, not to disrupt the inner-voice of Nero advising him, that was also one of the gestures' purposes.

Ruslan then spoke into a phone, and said, "Activate the alarm. There are three armed intruders in the command room on top of tower RK200. Engage with them and kill them. Whoever kills them first will be commemorated as a True People's Hero of the People's Soviet Empire, the highest honor of our nation. For the glory of our Great Leader", and thus in that exact moment, an amount only comparable to a couple dozen or so hundred P.S.E. cyber-ninjas were activated, and readied engagement-wise. They had not been doing much else on that base at the time, anyway, except for drinking vodka or smoking cigarettes. That was because the presence and testing of the highly secretive, highly dangerous technology that could influence the war considerably was in fact true, but that training had already concluded just an hour or so before, and it was now fit to be readily weaponized, although, admittedly, the weapon was only for the single use of Naydyr himself, and no one else, for it was too difficult and expensive to mass produce. It was so complicated and had so radically pushed the very boundaries of science that it was, roughly in estimation, probably worth, from all the engineering, experimentation, research and development, and everything of the sort, about two and one quarter trillion Soviet Rubles worth. So, you can understand why it couldn't be mass-produced, and was only meant for the Soviet Emperor's personal use.

Lyric, Joy, and Raven then all looked up to themselves, and saw that an alarm was going off and they had to fight their way out from where they had trapped themselves, unless they decided to jump out the window. Naydyr and Ruslan watched them on the cameras, which were closely following them, via invisible drones, that is, and as Naydyr watched them, he couldn't help but visualize a movie action scene, with accompanying intense, high-tempo music, that would play simultaneous to the graceful, seemingly artistic movements and attacks of Lyric, Joan, and Raven, all alike. Naydyr watched in admiration for how incredible Lyric was, his every swing of his blade, and dodge or side-step from gunfire, or his incredible aim and marksmanship, taking out dozens of P.S.E. cyber-ninjas all at once, continually.

He thought to himself, watching Lyric, saying, "This... this is the power of Lawrence of Arabia. The leader of the Arab Revolts, yes, this is his destiny, this battle!"

Lyric, having just sliced apart the chest of a Soviet

cyber-ninja, then became all the more alerted, in only just an instant, and looked frantically, and immediately relayed through the intercom to Joy and Raven, "The room's primed to explode, watch out!"

Naydyr then pressed a button on his desk, and the entire command room that the three of them were inside of, where the P.S.E. cyber-ninjas were flooding into like sacrificial omens to a god of blood after being met with the precision and skillfulness of fighting that these three Western warriors were capable of, was then made to explode, just to see what would happen, and to get a better view of them, to force them out into the open. They were in his trap, in his domain, in his house, in his country, they would have to play by his rules, he reasoned to himself with satisfaction.

All three of the Western warriors then leaped outward from the explosion, and Naydyr watched with incredible interest and dying attention, for his cinematic mind could only play the same intense, high-tempo song he had playing in his head from before, and this artistic streak, this proclivity to witness real life as if it were art, art to be appreciated and thought over, was his trademark Neronian influence, for Nero had been an awful emperor, and instead, an impassioned, disregardful artist.

And with the gracefulness of a calligraphy expert slashing across a white canvas paper, with the swiftest of strokes, the gentlest touch of exactitude, the most practiced, concerted, focused direction of energy, and expense of energy, Lyric leaped and jumped through the air, swinging his blade and firing his projectiles, being missiles and automatic gunfire, abounding from the floor and walls and platforms alike like a gazelle in the African countryside, taking a dozen P.S.E. cyber-ninjas on and engaging with them all and disposing of them just as quickly. He was, truly, the leader and veteran of the group, and it was a legendary performance for a warrior in all of the ages of war, where many past warriors watched through spirit form in complete disbelief and admirable jealousy.

Joy and Raven also were making slight work of the other attacking P.S.E. cyber-ninjas, and they were having an absolute slaughter. Joy was armed with her own sonically charged, ultra-sharp, English longsword-styled blade, as well as handheld submachine guns that could be holstered on her back, and Raven also had his own sonically-charged tactical sword as well, as well as his own guns too. All three of them were fighting all of them off, but Naydyr focused especially on Lyric, for he could perceive that he was the leader of the band of assassins, that he was the most skilled warrior. As Lyric dashed and swayed through the hail of bullet fire and attacks, and elegantly, with a degree of svelteness, Naydyr watched while replaying in his head that high-tempo song he thought would align up great with this picturesque scene, this lightshow of sparks and explosions.

Those three were at the bottom floors, the regular ground floor, whey they were fighting crazily at intense speeds. It was then that Lyric began to speak into his intercom. He said to the equally overwhelmed partners of his, Joy and Raven, "I just scanned the memory of one of these soldiers, while I was holding his detached head. Toad and Bear are located within the base, tucked away. They're probably watching us right now. What is that- What?"

It was then that a sudden howl in the air rang, and it was the sound of stealth bombers, several of them, a whole fleet, in fact, that then proceeded to airstrike the entire area, being the base, and thus completely annihilated and eviscerated every semblance of life or structure in the entire radius of the base, what was once Ukrainka Air Base, which was now unformed rubble.

The airstrike was one foul testament to the lunacy and utter madness of Naydyr and Ruslan's leadership, nobody could ever conceive or comprehend why a leader would airstrike their own base, especially when they knew it would likely not kill any of the three assassins, but rather, their own men. But it was classic. Classic behavior by the two numbskulls, who listened to voices in their heads as ultimate say on any matter. Complete and utter madness, an offense to God himself. The desecration and destruction of your own soldiers as well, was, in fact, reprehensible, too, for it begged the question, what honor did this military force have when it blew up its own, when it killed its own? Well, it was true, what they say, after all. There is no honor amongst thieves.

Lyric, Joy, and Raven all somersaulted and backflipped and barrel rolled out of the blast zones of the airstrike and were able to shield themselves from any harm. So, after all, the airstrike did not harm any of the assassins, wastefully, yet thankfully so.

Joy and Raven were exhausted, gasping for air, breathing with the greatest yearning of any semblance of a breath, after having flipped around for their very lives, while Lyric was the only one who was composed still like an ultimate soldier, an ultimate killing machine, and he proved his battle-tested, leadership rank, and he checked up on his two underlings, and said, "Joy, Raven, look up, at the mountain!"

It was Naydyr and Ruslan, who had emerged out of a crevice in the mountain overlooking the base, which had been eviscerated, and they looked over the exposed three, for these Western warriors were now out in the open, exposed and exhausted. They had both exited from being inside the base, through a deeper, underground tunnel which then led up to the mountain's opening, through a cave system, having been protected from the airstrike in their short migration.

Behind Naydyr and Ruslan were their trillion-dollar mech suits, which used anti-gravity propulsion technology to scar and tear through the air with possessed-like angles, like a UFO, like something terrifying you've never seen. They used these things like personal jets, to be quite descriptive, they were so efficient and speedy at traveling that they were used to go from one country, to another, staying in-between for however long, and all the such, all the while being able to travel whenever and wherever in record time. They required no maintenance to remain optimal in usage, and they truly were trillion-dollar mech suits, they were luxurious and awe-inspiring. Anyways, they were "parked", or left to remain dormant, in the mountain opening which they had landed upon, where they had entered the premises in the first place. Before, they had exited from their mechs, gone into the mountain opening and down through the deep underground tunnel, and then into the inner areas of the base itself, where they then had resided deep in the base, where they had watched the trio. Regardless, they were now looking down at Lyric, Joy, and Raven, and those three were looking up at them. They were separated by a considerable distance. It was a good enough distance to the point where you wouldn't realistically be able to even yell loud enough for one another to hear each other. That is how far of a distance it was, it was plenty far. Either way, the two parties could clearly define and see each other, looking out, and they were both transfixed on each other. Naydyr and Ruslan had their mechs a few meters away from them, on the mountain opening, but they were not actively going towards them, they were standing still, just watching the trio. The trio, with Lyric standing in the foremost position of the three, facing closest towards the direction of the duo, barked into his intercom to Joy and Raven, saying, "That's them, Toad and Bear."

Toad and Bear were the code names for Naydyr, being "Toad", and Ruslan, being "Bear". Naydyr was called Toad for his toad-like appearance, a fat neck, and large face. And Ruslan was called Bear for his large stature, and also for his Russian identity being connected to the other cultural name for the nation of Russia, being the "Bear."

"Should I shoot, Lyric?", Joy spoke out quickly and attentively, for the bloodshed she had committed had gotten her adrenaline running, and she was aiming her crosshairs on Naydyr's blurred silhouette, swaying in the distance.

But before Joy took matters into her own hands and sniped Naydyr, something unpredictable happened, yet again.

That was when a screechy, ringing, static-like noise began to occur in all of Lyric, Joy, and Raven's head. Joy and Raven grabbed their heads, attempting to ease this horrid headache, by rubbing their heads, for they were very, visibly, authentically shaken and affected by this noise. Lyric was the strongest, for he had just stared at the ground in a slight grimace, while his soldiers-in-arms were beside themselves. Lyric thought to himself, could this be the secret weapon? Perhaps a sonar, acoustic, or sound-type weapon, that was just used on them, he then reasoned and guessed.

"I know you have come to kill me", Naydyr then said through the spirit world, with his tone traveling through the spirit space, where his voice penetrated and subsided within the inner seats of consciousness in each of the three.

Lyric, Joy, and Raven then each fell to their knees, for they couldn't comprehend what sensation was overpowering them, this foreign invasion by Naydyr's consciousness, having broken into and having established itself firmly in each of their minds, their inner thought monologues, their own consciousnesses. And yet, this wasn't the full extent of this power, for not only did the trio hear Naydyr, but they felt a restraint, a choke, over their own selves, not allowing themselves to speak. But what they could do was visualize each other near each other, they could still close their eyes, and know they were still near each other, still near each other for support, for guidance, for the simple comfort that one may not be alone in death.

Raven, especially, felt as if he were about to die,

after being mind-hacked like that. He hunched over on his knees, trying to move up, to rise, to stand up, but he was caught in a paralysis, a gripping chokehold of terror and intrusion, that was freezing him, freezing his body and not allowing him to move at all. He was in agony the most out of the three, he was the weakest-minded and weakest-willed, rather substantially.

Richard of the Lionheart was pitying his future incarnation, watching over him, from the spirit world. He was being comforted by Joan of Arc, and Lawrence of Arabia was having a staring match with Nero.

Lyric, still writhing in pain and mental anguish from being neuro-shocked, was certain that this was the secretive experimental technology that was described by spies and informants, it was this mind-hack device, or system, that now Naydyr was wielding on them, he was certain that this was the technology. Lyric then saw his two soldiers-in-arms, being frozen as he was, and he looked up at the silhouettes of Naydyr and Ruslan, in the distance, and he knew he had to be strong for his two soldiers, his two hotshots, he had to be brave for them, it was up to him to set the tone of their response to this, it was up to him to inspire hope in them, he was the leader, he had to respond and act fast!

Lyric then raised his head, and yelled internally in his mind, assuming that was the correct way to communicate back to Naydyr's statement. He yelled, "For crimes against humanity, emperor Chanming, you have been declared appropriate for an extrajudicial killing, no trial would be appropriate for your resume. And kill you we shall", which took all the energy out of him to say, still not fully retaining control of his body, nor having exited his lethargic state. What was interesting though, however, was how both Joy and Raven were also able to hear what Lyric had thought, it was if the four of them, Naydyr and the trio, it was if they were all on the same channel together, that they could think and hear each other's thoughts. Hearing Lyric lash out back at Naydyr eased Joy and Raven's fear and nerves considerably, they each regained some semblance of confidence.

Naydyr, who was still only just a silhouette facing towards them over a great distance away, beamed back at them, answering Lyric's reply, and easing the paralyzing shock treatment on all three of them, allowing them to regain their composure. Naydyr only intended for them to talk for only a brief few more moments, he wasn't worried about any of them striking him.

His answer was simple, yet deep, and went completely over the heads of all three of this assassin team, and it was said with pity, and patronizing tough love, for he said, "You call me emperor, yet, you do not know what that means. You say you are to kill me, yet you do not first know who I am. You also do not know who you are, yourselves. But this… you do not understand."

Ruslan, who was also eavesdropping on the psychic conversation party, yet not revealing himself, laughed to Rasputin and himself after hearing what Naydyr said. He understood that he was referring to how Lyric had denounced him as this evil kingdom's emperor, while ironically being unaware that Naydyr, also, quite literally, was an emperor, in his past life. So, he called him an emperor while not knowing he was, yes, actually an emperor, the fullest sense of the word. Furthermore, he picked at Lyric's threat, asking him how he could want to kill him, yet he does not know who he is, truly, he would not even know who he would be killing. This, too, went over the trio's heads.

Joy, regaining her inner-strength, and finding the courage, then erupted as well back at Naydyr, proclaiming, "We know who you are, stupid moron."

Joy, while Naydyr and Lyric were engaging briefly, had been studying Naydyr's voice, upon hearing it so directly, so closely, as if the spirit world was a better connection than the physical world. As a woman, she sensed that Naydyr was an attractive man, a confident one, one who also possessed a degree of arrogance. She knew to sense this for she had dealt with male egos all her life being in the military, and through ascending the highest of ranks, she was all too accustomed to five-star generals, leaders, and the such, and their lofty opinions of themselves. She knew, from going off his voice, that Naydyr was a leader, a true leader, in the sense that he was destined to be this important. She also sensed a vulnerability in his voice, a hollowness, a sense of depression. It was her first time, the very first time, that she felt a humanization towards him, for he was always portrayed as a ruthless, unpredictable, psychopathic maniac. But no, she could also tell, most definitely, he was evil. Because when he spoke, he spoke, directing his words at your soul, not you. He did not expect you to understand what he said to you, because to him, you were below him, quite plainly. She pondered over the words he said to Lyric, that... they did not know who he was, and neither did they know who themselves were? It was confusing to her, she didn't know even one thing about the realness of past life consciousnesses and the such, and thus was the plight and curse of Naydyr, in a way, to be cursed with the alienating knowledge nobody else has. However, he did, after all, seek it out himself. This curse was self-inflicted. But if you asked him personally, he would tell you he never had the Free-Will to control that either way, it was Destiny.

Lyric and Raven then looked at Joy, who had just flung her insult at Naydyr, and Raven was scared, for he thought maybe they all were to be summarily executed as of that moment. It was Lyric who saw deeper though, into what had transpired, for he was proud of Joy, for he had predicted to himself that she would impress him especially, somehow at some point in this mission, and in that moment, she did, with her courage and bravery, and mental-strength to then vocalize herself, she was a real stand-out pupil. Lyric then looked at Raven, and he was still struggling to breathe. He thought to himself, what would this war have looked like without people like Joy, without people like himself? Because he knew, deep inside, being completely honest, that soldiers of Raven's caliber could never ever hope to win this war, not with the enemies being capable of things like this, not with so much secrecy and mysteriousness surrounding their weapons. Lyric then looked at Naydyr, who was still over a great distance away, and chuckled, having thought to himself that this mission had not gone anywhere near as planned, not beyond his wildest expectations, but still, it was not over, yet.

Naydyr looked down, and then thought in his head, relaying this message to the trio, "You call me a 'stupid moron', that is funny."

Lyric, Joy, and Raven all tightened up, in

anticipatory anguish, especially Raven, who was accepting certain death. And then, just like that, they felt the other-worldly, transient, force then take over their mouths and bodies yet again, and they couldn't move or speak, but only listen.

And to come clean, and be completely honest, the mind and body control as well as forcible telepathic connection were not, in fact, the secret, highly experimental weapon that the trio, especially Lyric, thought it was. For actually, the telepathic mind powers were simply another spiritual advantage that Naydyr possessed, having delved into the dark arts of occultism and energy projection so immensely and heavily. It was something he was always capable of, but rarely used, except for moments like this, for it expended a great deal of focus, and energy. You see, he took great interest in would-be assassins that came to kill him, for he liked to pick their brains apart a little bit, maybe converse with them once they were halted, perhaps even attempt in vain to relinquish some knowledge upon them. This, of course, was because of the vanity of Naydyr. He knew very well that these would-be assassins would have been briefed on all sorts of minute details about him, that they were tasked to obsess over him, and that to finally meet him... was to be the very most important time of their life.

Naydyr then continued to telepathically speak, saying, "Just know this, my friend. For this very day you talked to me... was, and always will be, the most important day in your entire life. And for me, today was just another Sunday."

Nero, Ruslan, and Rasputin all burst out laughing

at this disrespectful, dismissive quip.

Lyric, Joy, and Raven then felt enraged, for they felt humiliated and humbled beyond belief, especially Raven and Joy, who prided themselves on their military rank. Lyric, who had been focusing his strength concertedly, was able then again to break the transient force holding them all back, and he unlocked his speech in this telepathic connection they all had, planning to speak for all of his party, this disgraced, embarrassed, and disabled band of elite assassins.

Lyric then telepathically spoke triumphantly, erupting, having felt so disrespected and belittled, saying, "You will rot in Hell!"

Joy and Raven then felt exasperated, afraid, for their mission leader, their superior ranking commander, had just, in what barely ever happened, let an emotional outburst happen. Raven, who had been terrified this entire time, having made a little baby of himself, then recoiled into himself, for he then felt so strongly that they all would be executed, somehow, someway. Joy, on the other hand, had her heart broken, for the strongest man she knew and the only soldier comparable to her in terms of skill and accomplishments, was, in effect, reduced to a helpless, emotional wreck. This broke her heart into a million pieces, and she looked up into the sky, and it started to rain.

The raindrops fell on her face, as she began to have tears as well, intermingling with the rain.

She knew they had failed the assassination mission. They would not end World War III that day.

Nero snickered to Naydyr, "Show off your new toy already. That fool Lawrence of Arabia disrespected you today. He ought to know you do not disrespect an emperor."

Ruslan and Rasputin laughed again to themselves, and Naydyr raised his left arm, for on his left arm and extending onto his left hand, was a long, sleek, black glove. This glove, yes, was the secret, highly destructive weapon that was being developed there, at Ukrainka. Part of Naydyr's decision to airstrike the base to smithereens was also to destroy any data or records of the weapon too, it was simply that powerful of a weapon, this very glove was, so that its construction would be forever lost in time, incapable of ever being duplicated by anyone else. He had the one, there was no need for another in this world, he told himself. There was, after all, a stroke of genius to the madness.

Naydyr held an expressionless demeanor on his face, apathetic and tired. He was already bored of these three would-be assassins. They obviously didn't like him, he knew for certain, and for despite his admiration for their combat prowess, he still understood that they were still the enemy, he would have to show no mercy to them, as befitting of the tone and mood of the war's trajectory at the time. This could be his statement, yes, to the superiors that briefed and sent out this trio. He also felt like he had wasted himself, like he had with Sesto all those years ago, trying to allude to and enlighten the trio on the realness of this additional layer of reality that they were so ignorant to, and it was very obvious, it had all completely gone over their heads. He was disappointed, but not surprised. Disappointment seemed to be a common theme in his life, he reflected to himself, in his own solace. And alas, he raised his left arm, and hand, slowly, with his pointer finger particularly extended downward and progressively moving upward, very deliberately, and leisurely.

This was because Naydyr had noticed a single screw, a screw which could've been from a military grade vehicle that was destroyed by the airstrike, or perhaps part of a wall, or something, whatever it may have been, Naydyr noticed it, and he saw the sharpness of the edge, the cylindrical shape, ending at a corkscrewed sharpness, and how this could do serious damage to anyone if aimed at someone with a high speed.

This long glove on Naydyr's left arm and hand, yes, this was the secret, highly dangerous, highly valuable weapon that could sway the war considerably.

For as Naydyr raised his arm, with his finger, he was also raising the single screw off the ground as well, levitating it telekinetically!

The long glove that Naydyr was wearing gave him power over all metal objects, allowing him to levitate, float, or shoot out at an incredible speed, anything made of metal, and I mean anything made of metal, very aptly put. It was a telekinesis glove, that operated solely regarding metal objects, or mass composed of any metallic composition or structure. While wielding this glove, Naydyr could very well grasp and disarm anyone holding a gun, ripping it out of their hands with forces of insurmountable, unchallengeable strength. The origins and development of this telekinesis glove were unknown, and with the base it was developed at being utterly destroyed, there was no hope of ever learning how this terribly, frighteningly powerful weapon was created. Perhaps, it was reverse-engineered from alien technology, or perhaps it was reverse-engineered from inner-earth, advanced civilization technology, if that were to really exist, because when attempting to explain this very weapon, you would really put nothing past it, it was so remarkably inhuman.

And the screw rose and rose, standing upward, and as Naydyr slowly raised his pointer finger, the nail then calibrated itself, and pointed itself in the direction of the trio, who being so far away, could not even make out what was occurring in that moment.

Lyric, Joy, and Raven then regained control of their bodies, and Raven, being the most exhausted and drained mentally and physically, fell to the floor on his face. Joy hurried over to him, helping him regain his composure. She herself was equally as drained. It was Lyric, however, who was still kneeling in a pose not unlike that of an exploratory scout scouring the land, still focused on the silhouettes in the distance.

Lyric spoke into his intercom, in a desperate tone, saying, "Joy, Raven, are you alright?"

Joy looked at him to answer and reassure him that they were okay. And then, with the sudden crack of what could only be described as a feeling of absolute dread and terror, a lightning strike of utter fear, then overpowered the minds of all of them, had they not already been through enough. It was Naydyr telepathically reaching them one last time. He spoke a single word, with blank indifference. He then flicked his left index finger in the direction of the trio.

"Catch."

The sound barrier had been broken, just then, in that moment, and there was a sonic boom, echoing throughout the surrounding forests.

A whizz then occurred in the air, the sound of something flying at an incredible speed, a clean and precise noise, with expertly measured exactitude, yes, it was the nail, that Naydyr was telekinetically controlling, he had launched it at them, shooting it out like from the barrel of a gun, or better, the barrel of a tank, shooting a missile, for it flew at the speed of sound, almost instantly covering all the distance between the two parties in nanoseconds, flying through the rain, moving faster than the raindrops themselves could hit the ground.

The nail zipped with the grace of death, going straight through Lyric's cyber-ninja helmet, impaling and digging deep into his brain, creating an incision and wound so small and exact yet so fatally devastating, and then exiting through the back of his head, continuing to fly until it was lost in the ground behind them.

Lyric had been instantly killed. He was dead, slumping over on the floor, his body was lifeless. It was an instant kill, painless, and swift, and just as equally senseless. It was a display of Naydyr and Ruslan's indifference and disregard for human life. It was a very disrespectful execution.

Joy's mouth was agape, her expression was sheer shock, she could not believe it, her teacher, her commander, her fellow soldier-in-arms, her accompanying assassin, her training partner, her.... lover, was dead.

He was gone, just like that. Joy thought to herself, this man, who said, "Catch", before killing Lyric, he was the evilest man in the world, crueler and more sadistic than she could have ever hoped to imagine. And the grief, the sadness, the hopelessness, the pure sensation of defeat, the acceptance of failure, it dawned on her all at once.

She broke down, and she had tears flow down her face.

On the mountain top, Ruslan then said to Naydyr, "Let's leave. You should spare the other two, so they can spread your legend."

Nero offered his own thoughts as well, in Naydyr's mind, rather cruelly reflecting, saying, "Lawrence of Arabia is an absolute nobody in the grand scheme of history anyway. All those three are. Don't waste my time even looking at them any longer. Let us return to Moscow."

Naydyr looked down again, at his designer shoes, and his face was sullen. All he could think of was how Lyric was met with Lawrence in the afterlife, how his past life must've been congratulating him, welcoming him, for he had endured a true warrior's death, and how that must've been an overwhelming experience for him. Naydyr thought of how he had, in a way, delivered to Lyric the ultimate gift, an escape from this horrible world. He, himself, had hoped that Joy and Raven would think over what he had said to them before, and hoped they would one day understand. He wasn't confident, though, that that would happen.

And the Two Beasts then turned their back.

As they entered their trillion-dollar mechs, preparing to fly to Moscow, Ruslan couldn't help himself, as he said to Naydyr, "That Richard of Lionheart was quite pitiful, don't you think? A sorrowful display of cowardice", referring to how Raven was so seemingly unqualified for this type of mission. Naydyr scoffed slightly in response, he wasn't going to say anything else. He was in deep thought now, communing with Nero on what to do next, in this state of the war. The mechs then released a cloud of steam from their joints, and openings, and they levitated slowly, building momentum, and then they each shot out into the distance like black shadows.

It was still raining, and Joy's tears intertwined with the raindrops. She had removed her helmet now, and Raven was still on the fence of unconsciousness from exhaustion.

"Command, I need an evac at my coordinates. Lyric.... is dead. Raven.... needs immediate assistance. The mission was a failure", Joy said in a weakened, tearful tone, indicative of every ounce of pent-up frustration and impassioned defeat.

The rain baptized Lyric's body, his second baptism, one of death.

She didn't get the chance to tell him, tell him that she had wanted to marry him, after the war was over.

And Joy cried, and cried, and cried.

War was an evil thing.

CHAPTER 7

Surprise Party, Death and Rebirth

December 9, 2050, 9:39 PM

Payurov Military Base, Siberia, Russia,
The People's Soviet Empire

After ushering in the Dead Man's Hand Detonation Event, and exterminating almost all life on earth, Naydyr and Ruslan had then escaped in their mechs to Payurov Military Base, where an underground tunnel leading underneath the Arctic Ocean and beyond to where only God knows where, was hidden. They had planned on entering it soon, but thought to themselves, upon arriving, that they should stick around for a while, savor the earth that they believed they would be leaving, permanently, and bask in the air of their country, their homeland, their motherland, which they had, so perfectly in their minds, created with the greatest of consideration and thought. They had, in their minds, and amongst each other, to each other, become the single greatest men to ever walk the earth, the most influential, the wealthiest, the most powerful, and possessive of the greatest, or most infamous, legacy of any two leaders, ever, bar none, there was simply no debate, no contest.

They sat at the entrance of the base, smoking and sharing a couple of cigarettes. They were joking, and laughing, because everything had happened just as they thought it would've, just as Nero and Rasputin had told them, but they were not drinking any alcohol, not at that particular time, but they were thinking about it, considering it.

Since the P.S.E.'s territories and borders were not targeted by any of the Dean Man's Hand nuclear bombs, and remained largely untouched, aside from the already pre-existing ravages of World War III, there were soldiers already there at Payurov base, who had been stationed there for a while, having been tasked with managing the base's operations. The P.S.E. soldiers greeted the Two Beasts with much surprise however, they weren't aware that their two idols of unhealthy obedience and loyalty would, rather randomly and unannounced, show up to their rather tucked away, remote, usually laid-back base.

It was actually the greatest honor of any P.S.E. soldier's life to come in contact with, or to see in person, or to even glimpse a live appearance, of either Naydyr or Ruslan. For, after all, there were over four billion total soldiers in the P.S.E. armed forces, so the logistical odds, being just one soldier of so many, of ever even being located within a hundred miles of these Two Beasts was already very slim. This was a callback in history, actually, when Roman legionaries would be so blessed to ever glimpse their emperor. These two brutal kingdoms, Rome and the People's Soviet Empire, were very alike. There were both nations that were built to thrive off war. For Rome, it was highly effective for them in establishing their borders, and expanding upon it. For the P.S.E., they did the same thing, but on an exponentially larger scale.

Naydyr and Ruslan felt at ease, they felt comfortable. Which was amazing, in retrospect. They had just committed the greatest atrocity of all time on this cursed earth. They were dreaming of this moment for a while, and they had literally made it reality, for to them, they had "hacked" reality, they had "beaten" God, through synthesizing their own consciousness with that of their past lives, and they had done something absolutely unprecedented, something unthinkable, inconceivable, irreconcilable, the limitations of words and language could not adequately describe it.

But they forgot something. Or, rather, they did not know something, perhaps something they couldn't know.

This was something very important. And the soldiers conversing with Naydyr and Ruslan were smiling, having a glorious old time. They were unbelievably enthused to see their leader.

But this was because of something else entirely from them just being mere soldiers being starstruck encountering their superstar.

No, this was because these P.S.E. soldiers had,

because of the fabric of reality itself tearing from Naydyr's Dead Man's Hand Detonation Event, and in the same way that Joy had connected with Joan of Arc, synthesized with their past lives.

Yes, and this was not something Naydyr or Ruslan could've known, for they were so terribly self-absorbed, they could not fathom to even think of that being a possibility, for they already were naturally high and elated, twistedly, relishing in their own proof of their own wickedness. Quite simply, they weren't thinking of anything else, whatsoever. They could not have thought of other people accomplishing what they had, being the consciousness synthesis, for they were still not in an alert mindset. They thought they had beaten reality at that point, they had beaten God.

Which is never the case.

Ever.

That is one of the few truly impossible things.

So, as Naydyr and Ruslan were at ease, probably being rabidly congratulated by Nero and Rasputin, the very P.S.E. soldiers standing next to them, had in fact synthesized, most of them, with their past lives, and all of whom then understood as their divine, godly duty, was to unite against the Two Beasts; for it was now Team Humanity versus Team Naydyr and Ruslan.

Point, blank, period.

All it took was for two P.S.E. soldiers to accomplish synthesis, and then they could easily then persuade and regain liberty to a third soldier in the room, who maybe was not ready for their own synthesis, for whatever reason in their spiritual timeline. Thankfully, a majority of P.S.E. soldiers were, in fact, ready for synthesis, so this was never an issue to begin with, being a potential civil war between the misunderstanding un-synthesized and the saved, freed synthesized. Everyone was on the same page at this base, and they had known, from being told by their past lives, that Naydyr and Ruslan would be coming to the base after their atrocious act, a sin to the mother earth that united all people, of all lifetimes!

"No, really, I swear to you, I am a humble man, you wouldn't believe, I truly am a humble man, my comrade", Naydyr said in a slight angle of drunkenness, to a soldier he was conversing with, for right now, Naydyr thought of himself as the most legendary Communist Leader of all time, the most revolutionary of revolutionaries, a true man of the ages.

So why not get drunk for once?

Ruslan was drunk too, for you must understand, Nero and Rasputin's consciousnesses were equally unbeknownst to the trap they were in. They had no idea, for consciousnesses in the spirit world communicate on a one-to-one basis, just like in the physical world. So, it wasn't like there was some hivemind shared amongst the past lives that would enlighten or tip-off Nero and Rasputin of everyone else's plan, there simply wasn't.

"Comrade, you are so humble, truly. You are a man of the people, truly. My comrade, if you are so humble, can you please retrieve more cigarettes for us, in the bunker house? Please comrade, I myself am so drunk, I cannot. I would love to tell my children, my brothers, my parents, that the very own Naydyr Chanming, being so truly humble and such a lover of his people, retrieved my cigarettes upon my humble request, if you would do that, please, my comrade!", an impassioned P.S.E. soldier said to Naydyr, around the bonfire they were all sharing, gathering nearby.

This P.S.E. soldier was actually the reincarnation of the ancient Greek actor Polus of Aigena. Polus was a famous ancient Greek actor who was known for his skills in acting in tragedies. And here he was, reincarnated, acting so beautifully, in such a tragic sense, to the literal devil of mankind, so that he could be finally defeated. Polus would fulfill his ultimate destiny, literally acting, to save the very world, to vanquish the enemy, something not even the greatest warriors could do. You must understand, so many people and would-be assassins died in vain trying to eliminate Naydyr, and Ruslan, too. But here was but a humble actor, an actor in Greek tragedies, that was here, in this moment, ready to play the greatest serpent like an even better serpent himself, like a damn fiddle. His name, also, as a P.S.E. citizen, was Pava Agafonov. Pava Agafanov was Polus of Aegina. Oh, our God in this particular reality was so wonderful, in his incredible design and poetic angle to which life was designed from his genius.

Naydyr, in a deeply emotional, drunken state, revealed an extremely rare amount of emotion, for once, having felt so touched by Pava's deception, and by his communistic pride and self-idealization. He almost shed a tear of sheer emotion, from the fake connection he thought he shared with this soldier, Pava.

"My dearest comrade, I shall return shortly!", Naydyr said with a quickened disposition, leaving quickly as to hide his tears from the soldiers, and Ruslan, for this moment made him feel as if he was right all along, about everything, he felt in his heart, from Pava's deception.

Remember, it was Team Humanity versus Team Naydyr and Ruslan, at this point.

They intended to kill him, and they planned this very cruelly, for they were mad at him tremendously, and ashamed of themselves, for their own submission to his wickedness, and such, they felt the humanistic urge to redeem their lives, may they enter the Kingdom of Heaven, after all they had done, and complied with, being P.S.E. soldiers. Their plan was to make Naydyr go retrieve the cigarettes from the bunker house, which were actually there, and while he was making this short trip, they would aim a gun at Ruslan's head, telling him to be quiet, and force him to watch Naydyr get killed, this was their own personal irony, their own cruel concoction of a divine plan of justice. Naydyr would open the door from the bunker house, thinking he would simply make the short, being just a few short meters, stroll to the bonfire.

What would actually happen to him is that he would open the door, and be met with over a hundred P.S.E. soldiers aiming their guns at him. They were hoping to shock the life out of him. Also, to make matters even more remarkable, being that this was the very story they all reasoned that would be told for the rest of history, a most twisted and yet ironic plot twist that could only be true in real life, was that Joy Adelyn, Raven Leverette, Alaric Georgi, and Henry Cursor, were all going to be amongst the people aiming their guns at Naydyr. This was because they had all sneaked into the base in the middle of the day while Naydyr and Ruslan were already in a state of ease and relaxation. They sneaked in through the help of the newly synthesized and liberated P.S.E. guards. It was a team effort, Team Humanity at its best.

Team Naydyr and Ruslan had the rug pulled under from them, they had been finessed, they were tricked, duped, they thought they won, but something incalculably monumental had happened to stop them.

As Naydyr then scurried off, and out of sight, into the bunker house, all the soldiers and the remaining Western heroes then went into formation. Alaric and Henry then had Ruslan tied with very strong rope, and sat in a chair facing the bunker house door, and he also had a handkerchief stuffed in his mouth, so he could not alert Naydyr of the trap with his yelling. He had, quite literally, just experienced the greatest shock of his life, things went from zero to a hundred, really quick. He was still dumbfounded, and confused, and utterly terrified. There was no way the Soviet Emperor of the People's Soviet Empire would ever go out like this, no, he could not die like this, they could not die like this, he couldn't accept it!

To make matters even worse for the Two Beasts, as monks such as Rasputin know, to be capable of psychic powers, the powers that Ruslan had used on Sesto, earlier, for reference, you must most assuredly have abstained from any alcohol of the sort. This was simply how it worked, being its effects on the body, and now Ruslan, having been drunk at this point, could not escape under any capacity from his restraints with any powers, he was totally and utterly powerless, he had been played!

And then it happened, Naydyr swung open the

door of the bunker house, with the cigarettes in his right hand.

The Right Hand Path had defeated the Left Hand Path, in the end.

Truly, our God is a poet.

His eyes widened, and he sobered up, very, very quickly, in the mind, that is. In his body was still the alcoholic concentration, which was already higher than Ruslan's, so he himself was also not capable of any of his own psychic powers that he had honed through Ruslan's guidance, not any of the telepathy he used on Lyric, Joy, and Raven, or anything else. To make matters worse, the glove which created a telekinetic power over all metals, that weapon was also long since gone, having been lost earlier in the war.

Naydyr was done for. He had over a hundred rifles and guns aimed at him. He had no powers ready for him to use. He could not hide behind terrible technologies anymore. He was the serpent of all times, and yet, here, in this moment, he was trapped, he was unprepared, he was exposed.

He was at their mercy.

Nero screamed in Naydyr's head, "No! You've been betrayed by your own people just like I was! No! Not like this!"

"He's the devil, he's the devil!", a soldier screamed.

"Murderer!", an additional soldier yelled out.

"Don't let him talk!", Joy shouted out, aiming her rifle at his chest.

There were over a hundred laser beams, being under-barrel attachments on everyone's guns, pointed at Naydyr's body, but none at his face, or head. Raven had explained to the P.S.E. soldiers, his new brothers and sisters in humanity, that he wanted his head in-tact, to hang in his office. Joy remembered him saying this, shortly before they had stormed the bunker earlier that day, and she thought it was remarkable how, what she originally perceived as a sly joke, or remark, was now about to become the legend of humanity.

Ruslan, tied up, and gagged, sat in the chair, with complete terror and frustration, and made eye contact with Naydyr, and all Naydyr could see in his lifelong best friend's eyes was sorriness, being sorry for not protecting his brother, his leader, his emperor.

All the soldiers had an animalistic, tribal energy about them. This was a barbaric action, an uncivilized event, a death by firing squad, that is what it essentially was. But to them, it was necessary.

Naydyr, then looking away from Ruslan, and to Joy, having eyed over all of his former subjects, and having even noticed, shockingly, the Americans, then opened his mouth to speak, and he said, "I, I—"

And Joy, having stuck to her word, did not let him finish talking, she wouldn't risk it, she wouldn't give him the chance, the opportunity to speak, to maybe persuade his soldiers, or to bide his time, no, she would kill him, now, and avenge her lover and hero, Lyric Abdiel.

She then shot her rifle straight at his chest, and the bullet ripped and went right through his body, exiting out from behind his back. This was Joan of Arc's ultimate destiny, which Joy would carry out, it was their destiny, together, to defeat the final enemy of humanity. And he coughed up some blood, but still stood. He tried to formulate some words, but before he could, he was choking on his own blood.

The other soldiers were shocked, that someone had actually fired already, but they knew, from the dialogue with their past lives, that this woman was the famous Joan of Arc, she was a trailblazer, a true leader, and then they realized, they ought to shoot him too! Everybody gets a piece of him; everybody gets a claim to fame!

"Kill him!", Raven cried out, and Ruslan, who was forced to watch, was shedding tears profusely, shaking violently in his chair. And yet, it was ironic, for the singular death of one man meant infinitely more to him than the slaughter of a vast majority of the world at large. Same with Naydyr, who felt nothing from the nuclear annihilation. A particular, special Holy Man from two thousand years ago did say it best, after all, when he said, "Those who live by the sword, died by the sword." And these two men had been murderers, and thus, they were destined to be murdered, if you would concede to that tenet of life, and how Karma works.

All the soldiers then let their guns go wild, spraying Naydyr up, riddling him with bullets, including Alaric, Henry, Joy, Raven, and all the P.S.E. soldiers, and Naydyr's body twitched and spazzed from the volley of bullets coming from all directions in front of him, and he was all bloodied, his whole outfit covered in his leaking blood, spilling all over himself and the floor. He croaked a little bit, trying to conjure up any semblance of any word, but his neck and trachea had been shot, his voice-box had been destroyed, he was unable to speak anymore.

Oh, how poetic, the serpent himself with the Voice of the Dragon would never speak again.

The over a hundred or so former P.S.E. soldiers and the four Western warriors all had fired each at least five shots, or two bursts or so, of bullets into Naydyr's body, all over him, from his legs to his arms, to his stomach to his thighs, there were bullet holes and gaping wounds all over him now. Ruslan was beside himself. After all of them had stopped shooting, they stood in disbelief, they looked at Naydyr, whose entire body was painted red except for his face, save for his mouth, which was all bloodied, having been profusely leaking blood out of it, for Naydyr's innards and bodily composition was ravaged, and destroyed, being his organs and the such.

But he was still standing, somehow, even though he was shot over 300 times, roughly, in total.

He stood, in a crooked way, since his back was shot through, and his posture was barely indicative of whatever could be considered a legitimate stance, but he was not hunched over, he was still upright, barely. And he was breathing very heavily, very shallowly, for his lungs were punctured, and his windpipe destroyed, he was a living, breathing corpse, at this point. Surely, he was just a dozen or so seconds from falling over and dying.

But he still stood, and something very terrifying began to happen to him.

All the soldiers and Joy, Raven, Alaric, and Henry, watched in horror, and utter disbelief, for Naydyr started to convulse, and shiver, and shake, and squirm in his body, in his frame, and it was not unlike that of a typical exorcism, the way he was moving, unnaturally, with his joints, and his limbs. He was almost having a seizure, it looked like, all while standing up.

What could command this movement, in a man whose body was utterly destroyed?

How was he still standing?

Alaric wondered these things to himself, as he studied him with the eagle eye of Alexander.

But what Joy noticed, was that his face, his expression, was that of equal terror to that of the witnessing soldiers, it was as if Naydyr himself had no idea what was happening to him either. In his eyes, he looked deathly scared, as if he couldn't control his body, he couldn't control any part of himself, what little eviscerated, bullet hole ridden body of his that was left.

"Nero! Nero! What is happening to me? Nero! Help me!", Naydyr cried out in agonizing despair in his mind, but he did not receive a response, and this was very, very rare.

For what was happening was another event that was unprecedented in human history, for it could've never happened before, with the veil between the spirit world and the physical world having been intact, before this very day. It was another consequence of the Dead Man's Hand Detonation Event, that it had freed Satan to come into the physical world, on his own, in his own essence, for nothing was holding his accursed powers back anymore. This was the double-edged sword, the unfortunate, but balanced, opposite, angle to the great positivity of the enlightenment of the human race, as all things must be balanced, in good and bad. And thus, in the triumphant unification of divine justice, in the formation of Team Humanity, as was ordained by God, Satan would also have his final trump card, his final response, his final attack.

"Nero! Nero! Help me!", Naydyr panicked in his mind, and yet there was no response from Nero.

Rather, Naydyr heard a vaguely familiar voice instead, one he had not heard in almost fifteen whole years.

"Hello, Naydyr."

It was Sesto's voice.

Sesto Latif.

And Sesto's voice radiated a newfound devilishness, something completely uncharacteristic of the meek, nervous, timid Sesto that Naydyr had invited to his wedding, the Sesto that Naydyr invited to Gatchina Palace, so long ago, the young man who was so considerably younger than him.

"No…. who are, what, what is this? Where is Nero? Sesto, what the hell?", Naydyr replied back, while he was still convulsing erratically, and demonically, as if he was becoming possessed. This whole exchange, was, after all, only a duration of maybe, six or seven seconds, and the onlookers, this audience of his, were still frozen in disbelief and momentary awe.

And frozen is what they became even more, for

Naydyr's bloodied designer shoes then began to lift from the floor!

He was rising into the air, without the use of any technology, nor psychic powers, he was being raised by Satan himself, by the demonic influence and powers of Satan, which had finally been freed into the world. All the blood spilled by Naydyr as well then was raised, and levitated into the air as well, and it was pouring back into him, sucking back into his wounds, and his wounds were closing, and healing, and his seizure-like exorcism was diminishing to a more composed, intelligent, controlled posture. What the onlookers, the audience of this Satanic ordination, could not see, was that of Naydyr's soul being overtaken by that of Satan's. In the invisible, spirit world, Naydyr's soul body, his divine light body, which he possessed as a creation of God, no matter how despicable he was, was being infected, swarmed over, overtaken by the soul of Satan. Naydyr's soul's color was a golden yellow, actually, harkening back to Nero's original claims that he was the sun god Apollo incarnate, and Satan's soul was a dark red. And thus, this darkened red hue was continually overwriting this golden yellow, on Naydyr's light body, gradually, and quickly, replacing the golden yellow with its dark red.

His body was becoming Satan's. He was losing control not only of his own physical body, but also his own soul. This was, perhaps, why Naydyr could not hear Nero anymore, for Nero had been kicked out, removed from Naydyr's seat of consciousness, and replaced with Satan's voice.

"You really thought I was Cupid?", Sesto said to Naydyr, in the most diabolical, awful voice, as if he was speaking to a mere plaything, this meager tool of his being Naydyr.

"You fool, 'Cupid' does not even resemble the name 'Sesto' in any way, haven't you caught on by now, you little fool? You were named 'Naydyr', and you are Nero, 'Ruslan' is Rasputin, 'Joy' is Joan, I could go on. And yes, 'Sesto'.... was Satan", Sesto said with mighty disrespect to the feeble, afraid, powerless Naydyr.

It was quite ironic, quite fitting, how Naydyr had idealized himself as the truest representation of the devil on earth, that he was aligned with the devil, in his mind, and that the devil was empowering him, that they were on the same team, and yet, upon finally encountering the actual Devil, Satan, his idol of self-idealization did not care for him one bit, he did not respect him one ounce, he did not even wish to speak to him, what was to him a lowly human, a complete and utter fool, a little boy to him, at that.

Sesto Latif... was in fact, Satan's apparition on earth.

And when Naydyr had invited Sesto to his wedding, and then later to Gatchina Palace, Satan was playing "stupid", or playing "dumb", as one might say. He was operating undercover. Sesto, or Satan, was in fact, in all actuality, checking up on his little project, his little muse, Naydyr Chanming. Naydyr had presented himself to Satan as the perfect candidate to nuclearize the world, and then to have his body taken over. When Naydyr had read the excerpts from the ancient scriptures to Sesto, it was really him proving to Satan that he was really going to follow through with everything Satan had planned for him, to become his little tool, his own instrument of destruction.

The reason that Satan had appeared in the form of Sesto, and did not approach Naydyr directly, was because Satan had been imprisoned away from entering the consciousnesses of other humans, other mortals, and thus he necessitated a disguise, being Sesto Latif. But now, now that the barrier between the physical world and the spirit world had been shattered, which was exactly a part of Satan's master plan, Satan then could depart from Sesto and then enter Naydyr.

To clarify, Sesto had always been Satan, he was never a real person. The physical Sesto that the world knew as a musical artist, was in fact, what was most closely comparable to a shapeshifter, an apparition, an illusion, and not a real human. And once the nation of France, where the façade that was Sesto supposedly resided, was obliterated in the Dead Man's Hand Detonation Event, the "Sesto" we all knew simply evaporated into thin air, and traveled back to the spirit world, from where he then traveled, through the spiritual space, to Payurov Military Base, where he then watched as Naydyr was shot up, from behind the shadows, in a higher dimension. From this weakened, vulnerable state that Naydyr was then in, Satan was then able to overpower Nero and kick him out, and then infect and take over Naydyr's consciousness like a virus.

It was then that Naydyr's body was a full several meters floating off the ground, and his skin and flesh was perfectly healed, and was now a deathly, porcelain white. His eyes were completely black, save for a singular red dot of energy in the center where his pupils once were. His clothes, having been ripped to shreds, had also somehow been reconstructed as well. He was also in a messiah-like pose, with his arms spread outward, as if he had finally fulfilled his role as the false messiah, the Destroyed of this World. And the soldiers and Western warriors all looked in terror, and many had dropped their guns, attempting to run away as fast as they could. The anticipated victory they all had so passionately envisioned was now so far away. All the while, Naydyr's golden yellow light body, parallel to his physical vessel, in the spirit world, was now entirely dark red, there were no semblances or traces of any golden yellow anymore. It was true, then, that Naydyr and Satan had swapped places, consciousness wise, as well, and that Naydyr was now in Hell, where we would wake up shortly, and Satan was now in the physical world, with his own superpowered host, his own vessel, which he then held complete control over. The eyes in Naydyr's face then straightened out, for they had rolled back into his head, and the evilest smirk of all time, quite literally, was fully abound across the possessed, hijacked Naydyr's face, for this was Satan's property now.

Satan then, with his arms outwards, then recoiled them back, into his chest, and then with newfound momentum, exploded them outwards, and all the 300 or so bullets that had removed themselves from his body then shot outward, at the audience of onlookers, and a dark reddish hue of energy surrounded Satan, and his new body, and this energy, this plasma, this force field, was so strong it started to disintegrate and wear away everything near it.

But just in that instant, as the bullets flew outward at the former P.S.E. soldiers, at Joy, Raven, Alaric, and Henry, who were hopelessly stunned in complete disbelief, having dropped their guns, ready to run away for their lives, with their mouths wide open, something incredible happened, something equally responsive to Satan's physical entrance to this world.

Joy screamed.

"Jesus!"

"Jesus is here!

"Jesus has returned!"

CHAPTER 8

A Short Excursion in Hell

Eternity

The Lower Echelon of Hell

Naydyr had passed out, his consciousness had faded to black, for when he was so desperately fighting Satan's takeover of his own consciousness, it had transported him to where Satan was, in Hell, and they had each swapped places, with Satan in Naydyr's body, on earth, and Naydyr being sent to Hell, not in his own body, but in spirit form.

He had awakened, but he was not in Payurov Military Base, in Siberia, no, he was in complete darkness, there were no distinguishable objects or features in front of him, he could not make out any semblance of anything, anything at all. Naydyr felt a strange sensation, for he was not totally familiar with being in pure, true spirit form. He was, after all, a psychic power practitioner, and an occult expert, but very rarely had he ever experienced out-of-body trips, very seldom had he ever spent prolonged periods of time in his spirit form. In this spirit form, he still retained a body, arms, legs. He could also still feel pain, and touch, for the rules and stipulations of Hell were that you would experience physical and mental torture for your wicked deeds. Furthermore, you would not experience these sensations in your earthly, physical, mortal body, but rather in your spiritual body, which was actually more true, more real, more visceral in sensation.

Then, all of a sudden, a great illumination had occurred, and Naydyr could see the ground, and the foreground, and his surroundings. It was that of a circular, dome-like arena. The lighting was that of reddish, and fiery. Naydyr then knew, he was in Hell. The walls were made of marble, a particular marble that evoked an antiquated, antediluvian architectural design, from before the Great Deluge, older than the Noah of the Ark.

And it was then that the same song he had played in his head when he had so disrespectfully stepped on the Dead Man's Hand detonation button, the gradually building, intense song he had recorded a music video for, which he had thought of in his head before he set ablaze to the world, this very song had then begun to play in the arena Naydyr was in, but in a chopped and screwed sounding way, a distorted and demonic rendition of it, that was slower, and eviler. This confused Naydyr, and then all of a sudden, a microphone, which seemed so out-of-place in this area, had then materialized into his hand, a microphone for singing, for performing, not atypical of what a stage performer would have. It had manifested out of thin air, and placed itself in his left hand. It seemed so out of place, this earthly device, in this arena of Hell.

Crack!

"Ah!", Naydyr screamed in agony.

For a miniature sonic boom had then occurred, the crack of a whip. For Naydyr was then struck with a gigantic whip, in the back, and he fell over, having dropped the microphone, becoming horribly scarred on his back, and incredibly disoriented and overall afflicted with terrible pain and soreness.

Still sprawled across the floor, he then looked behind him, and in the darkness, he could see the legs of a gigantic, enormous, approximately fifty foot being, a demon of Hell, who only his lower body was visible, for he was sitting in an incredibly, equally as imposing, throne, or chair. His upper body, and face and head, were hidden in shadow.

This terrified Naydyr greatly, and he was filled with more fear than he had ever experienced in his life, being pure, real, absolute terror.

He was so puny before this fifty-foot-tall demon, this Lord of Hell.

Naydyr then stood up on his own, groggily composing himself, and he felt another force against him, this time it was a strong wind, as if someone had pushed him, or if the gigantic demon had blown at him, with his mouth. Naydyr was then blown over, carried away as if he was in a tornado, over back to where the microphone had fallen beside him.

The music now that he had been thinking of when he destroyed the world, just that very morning, was now playing louder and louder, building up until the part with vocals, it was a rap song after all, one that he had written himself.

Before Naydyr could even think to himself any semblance, any hint of a reaction to what was happening, the gigantic whip from the giant demon in the shadows cracked again, and Naydyr howled out in agony, but no sound came out, nothing but a hollow, strained gasp of air. No, he could not formulate any noise, no words, only the lyrics of the song he had written. It was clear to him, he was to perform this song, with the microphone in hand, or he would be whipped again, he would be tortured again. He then grabbed the microphone, and stood up straight, as if the demonic forces around him were stringing him along like a puppet, and the song had picked up by then, and he began to recite, or rap, the lyrics. Around him, he could hear the faint whispers and traces of chatter, as if the denizens of Hell had been waiting for his live performance, his arrival, to what he, at that point, accepted as his permanent new home. Tears flowed down his face, as he danced, and rocked side to side, reciting the lyrics to the tempo of the song, the song he had written when he was much younger, songwriting being one of many of Naydyr's lesser-known artistic proclivities, yet another imprint of his Neronian influence.

As he continued to rap along the song, he would experience flashes in his mind, from the perspective of his original body, which Satan had stolen from him forcibly, and he knew, deep inside, he had failed his mother, he had failed his father, he had failed his wife, his country, everyone in the world, he was an absolute blotch, a scrape, a scar on the timeline of humanity. This all rushed to him, as he could see himself fighting a white apparition, briefly, which he could not make out. But as he rapped the lyrics to his song in front of the crowd of accursed souls destined to writhe in Hell's flame for eternity, he could not believe it, for the nihilistic and dark lyrics he had written, had, after all, in the end, been so ironically fitting for this very moment.

The song then, in its duration, had come to a deliberate pause, to switch up the melody, and pace of its progression. And in that brief pause, Naydyr felt relief, that he could stop rapping, but he was then whipped again. Having raised himself up, again, with the slightest trace of remaining strength and lifeforce, he looked up and saw that the dome-like arena he was in, had now, no more walls around it. In its place was an open, ever-expanding view of infinite distance, and infinite fire, limitless fields of torched humans, little shadows and silhouettes that resembled bodies of people, running frantically and rolling around on the ground, desperately attempting to put out the fire consuming them, and it was a hellish scene, a disturbing and heart-wrenching visual.

"Emperor! My emperor!", a mostly disintegrated and zombie-like P.S.E. soldier then said, having appeared behind Naydyr, crawling on the ground, without a lower body, and having had grabbed his leg, with his left hand, which only had three or so fingers on it, where the opposable thumb served as the clinch for his other two fingers.

It was apparent, for the hundreds of millions of Russian and Chinese young men that had died in the namesake of Naydyr Chanming's royal Soviet majesty, had in fact, been a vast amount of the burning bodies around him. The song then picked up again, after its brief interlude, its brief pause in the track's instrumental, and Naydyr was to then finish up the rest of the song, rapping it, bar for bar. He got more into it, admittedly. He was making motions with his arms, his hands, and rocking his head back and forth. Naydyr figured to himself, if this was his ultimate destiny, to be a music performer before an audience of the damned, then he ought to do it like the earthly Naydyr would've, with concerted effort and excellence.

His whole life then flashed before his eyes, the decisions he had made, all throughout his earthly time, his spoiled childhood, his tumultuous youth as a teenager, and young adult, and his lengthy, controversial, polarizing career as a politician and leader. He especially remembered the people who had raised him, his grandparents, and his father, and he regretfully wondered if he had been denied a reunion with them, if they were in Heaven, without him.

His father had told him once, "If you're getting paid five dollars for the job, do seven dollars' worth of work."

Naydyr's mind was racing, he had hoped his enthused cooperation would perhaps grant him the privilege of escaping Hell, but he knew this was a pipedream.

He also remembered what his grandfather had also once told him, "If someone offers you a gift, never refuse it. Because if you do, that person will never give you a gift again. Why would they? You refused their generosity once before."

In his soul, Naydyr then felt a little thankful, for he wasn't burning in the fire, instead, rather interestingly, he was atop a stage of sorts, performing a song.

He had been blessed, by the standards of his predicament, albeit not in the way you would think, but his time in Hell so far had been mild compared to the other compatriots of his in eternal damnation.

He had finished up rapping his song, and then he felt a hand on his left shoulder, which was warm.

This touch felt familiar.

CHAPTER 9

The Final Chapter of History

December 9, 2050, 11:11 PM

Payurov Military Base, Siberia, Russia,
The People's Soviet Empire

It was time I revealed myself, and entered the fight.

As soon as the bullets flew outwards at Joy, Raven, Alaric, and Henry, as well as the P.S.E. soldiers, even including Ruslan as well, I then emerged from a portal I created, that did not lead from the spirit world, but rather the Kingdom of Heaven itself. This is why I could enter this physical reality with my own flesh and blood, my own tangible body, for I was not coming from the spirit world, I was not merely a spirit, I was flesh and blood, having come from another land of flesh and blood, not one of spirits. Yes, the Kingdom of Heaven was real, and it was physical. Perhaps, we could all relax later there, and reflect on this adventure, all of us, those who would be ready to enter, but alas, in this moment, I had to take care of a certain familiar enemy. I flew out the portal, at an incredible speed, and time was moving in slow motion for everyone around, a short, residual effect of the portal I had opened. Quite dramatically enhancing.

I looked at Satan, possessing Naydyr's body, and he looked back at me, scowling. I looked at the audience to this divinely ordained event, this divine orchestration, this battle, and I could see nothing but absolute relief in their faces, and tears, and smiles, and an unstoppable joy. It was remarkable, for they were entirely focused on me, and not Satan. They were not even phased nor perturbed by the bullets, which, moving in slow motion, I was then able to stop, by quickly placing a protective force field around everyone, including Ruslan.

Ruslan, who's tears had ceased, was in particular awe of me. I knew, that he would apologize for his ways, later. I looked forward to rebuilding our relationship, Ruslan and I. I know that he was, inside, a loving man, who loved his wife. That was proof he was still redeemable, like everyone else. And for Naydyr, I then knew that Satan had swapped their places, having hijacked Naydyr's body and placing him in Hell. I knew he had to remain strong, down there, in that place.

But I knew he would be, so I was not worried.

Some alone time would be good for him, wouldn't you agree?

But with all the onlookers all protected in their force fields, which I set to last the entire duration of this battle with Satan, I then knew I had to put on a show for everyone, that was, before I put an end to this evil in this world that had persisted for so long, for too long. It was hard, to stand back, and to watch, but our Father assured me, the time wouldn't be right until now, and now, I feel he was right.

"Jesus! Jesus! Jesus! Jesus Christ has returned! Jesus is here to save us!", screamed Pava with ecstatic enthusiasm, he was practically leaping in excitement and pure, unadulterated happiness.

Pava, one of my most beloved.

Satan, then, using his highly peaking dark powers, manifested out of thin air, an eastern styled blade in his left hand, which he then snapped his right fingers, and the eastern styled blade was then lit ablaze with a vermillion red, mesmerizing flame. It was, in all actuality, the sharpest blade that ever-seen exposure to the air in this very world.

It was then that I felt it must've been necessary for me to up the score, so to speak, I wasn't about to let the big bad guy show me up in front of these earnest believers, and so I opened my mouth, and a western styled blade extended out of my mouth, and fell into my right hand, where I then blew some of my breath onto the blade, and it then glowed with a golden luminosity, a divinely-inspiring brightness, like the sun itself, for the Son of God himself to wield. Yes, these details were important to me, for when you're Jesus, you can't disappoint. Not that you would either way, though. Regardless, I had enchanted my blade, just as Satan had his, and now my sword was the sharpest that had ever seen the exposure of the air, sharper than his. How about that one-up, huh, Satan?

He then leaped at me, and I leaped at him.

Our blades clashed, and sparks and lights flew abound, sparks from the intermingling of our enchantments on our blades, and the swinging of the blades left a trace effect in the air, and we painted a scene together, in the sky. We were leaping all over the snowy landscape of upper Siberia, a beautiful and picturesque setting for a battle such as this, and heavy loads of snow was being thrown and displaced everywhere, from when we each touched the ground, which was only for an instant, as we both maintained minimal contact with the ground, having been flying in the atmosphere with the utmost grace of a dragonfly in a lily pond. Satan leaped at me with the speed and vehemence of a cannon ball having been launched out of a fifty-ton cannon, and I answered back with the speed of a leopard at full exertion, but airborne, slicing and cutting the very wisps of air before me. I admired his skill with the blade, and he returned this respect, for he did not overdo his attacks, and neither did I.

Satan smirked, having leaped back from a clash of blades, and said with a very sarcastic tone, "Had to spoil my little party, Son of God?"

I answered back, "Well, you had to spoil my little planet, first, to be totally honest, Red Dragon."

This banter was to be expected, from Satan. He was, after all, the utmost patron figure of all disrespect.

For you see, higher ethereal-existing beings, that were ancient, and at this point, considered more primordial than anything, such as myself, Jesus Christ, and him, Satan, we were jokesters, we saw the humor in everything, our minds and our consciousnesses did not exist at the same level as humans, we weren't as detached from the moment, the present, we weren't lost in our heads, our inner-monologues, negative-thought patterns, no, we were one with the closest microsecond to the moment, that was, after all, what made us, what could only be accurately conveyed as... gods.

"Tell me, Son of God, how beautiful I look? How fabulous this particular vessel is, how perfect it is, how wonderful it looks", Satan said to me, which wasn't outside of his character, he was, after all, the embodiment of all that was to do with vanity and self-centeredness.

I looked at him, and his face, and leaned my head to the right. He loved to banter, this accursed accuser, this ancient character. Our last encounter was more or less the same, and the one before that, in that barren desert, so long ago, two thousand years ago. I decided not to entertain his self-aggrandizement, I had to make quick work of him, so that I could go and save Naydyr already.

Satan, visibly disappointed and unamused by my non-reciprocating mood towards his petty remarks, then opened his mouth, and like the great Red Dragon he was, he bellowed out a swarm of mesmerizingly wine-red fire, an otherworldly inferno, having instantaneously melting significant portions of snow and ice separating us. I then somersaulted, and backflipped backwards a great deal of distance, perhaps many dozen or so meters, and then aligning my life force, my Chi, like the Tibetan monks, I blew out a brazenly fierce, pure and equally sizeable, appropriately matching, stream of clear blue water, which then clashed and met the projected inferno with tremendous force, shaking the very tectonic plates beneath us. This then created an overwhelmingly enveloping sea of mist, and steam, from the collision of these two elements, fire and water. It was in this mask of mist that Satan's enchanted, fiery blade then poked out of the poor visibility, aimed right at my head, and I dodged it with the slightest of side steps. His blade shot out, slicing through the veil of mist, like a piston in a well-oiled machine, like an uppercut from an undefeated boxer with 17 straight knockouts. And so, I teleported behind him, a power and capability that I had been saving, for on this lower dimensional plane, and with myself being the ordained Right Hand of God, I was readily proficient at manipulating matter and space, on an atomic level. I vanished, and reappeared out of thin air, and swung my own blade of divine light at him, and rather disturbingly, his head and neck then rotated backwards like an owl would, and his arms seemingly popped out of his joints, and his fiery blade met mine, and this clash rang out and echoed through the air, causing the seldom birds who had gathered around the ledges and rooftops of Payurov Military Base to then fly up and fly away.

We then exchanged clashes of our blades rapidly, and with vehement force and indignation, Satan brandished his weapon, his extension of his body, with the whole magnitude of all the Sin in world history, with all the wickedness and depravity of every shortcoming of every grown man who fell prey to his lust, every young adult who failed in the face of temptation, of all the negativity and self-destruction in all the eras combined, for all the atrocities committed by the kingdoms of Nimrod's Babylon, Caesar's Rome, and all the future iterations of mankind's impulse to enslave and behead their fellow men, yes, this was entirely comprised into the destructive might of Satan, in this very moment.

And in return, I deflected his horizontal slices and vertical swipes with my own divine blade, which I also wielded with all the righteousness, all the mighty justice, the upstanding loyalty and devotion of God, which was present in the hearts of all the soldiers who sacrificed themselves to protect their nation's borders, and with all the earnest devotion of every just man who loved their lovers, and would do anything for them, with all the blessings and peacefulness of every white dove symbolizing the peace and life that our Father breathes unto us, and with all final breaths of every burned martyr who died in both my own and my Father's name, yes, all this energetic charge and divineness was present in me in this moment.

Having then sidestepped a close slash, I was then able to swing upwards, and slice both of Satan's very hands off, from each of his wrists, severing what was once Naydyr's very hands from his arms. It was then that his sword, still in his left hand, fell from his possession, for he no longer had it equipped, and it fell to the ground, falling hundreds of meters down to eventually fall into the snow, for we were both, in this moment, airborne in the atmosphere, honed in under a backdrop of northern lights, of a beautiful green and blue borealis.

We then both landed on the ground, and Satan then, in the manner of a lizard, or a chameleon, then regenerated both his hands, having restored himself.

What he did not do, however, was grab his sword again, opting not to re-equip himself. Instead, he smirked, and composed himself into an Asianic, martial art styled stance. He was prepared to fight me, yes, with his bare hands, with his bare might, for he was incredibly vain, and wanted to put on a show, before his estranged Father, who yes, was also his Father after all, too.

"Care to dance with me, Son of God?", Satan snickered, having powerfully set his legs into the ground, making a rigid, yet readily agile, stance. In this stance, he was ready to pounce, like that of a tiger. His arms then motioned like that of a grandmaster of the art of combat, and it was apparent, he had intended to fight me in hand-to-hand combat.

I then thought to myself, well, how pitiful of a display would it be before the many spirits watching, our audience of the multitude of souls, for me to fight a barehanded combatant with a weapon. No, that was not my way, that was not the way of the King of Kings, the Lord of Lords, no, I would entertain this challenge, I would defeat him at his own game. I then threw my sword to the ground, with its sharpened point then impaling the snowy layered ground, having placed its blade solidly in the earth like an incision into a wound of its own.

Having formed my own personalized fighting stance, which was most closely representative of Jeet Kune Do, one of my personal favorite idealizations, for its reference to water, and the movement of water, I then readied myself to engage in physical combat.

A single cry, a whistle, from a bird then echoed through our battlefield, and we both leaped at each other, having met each other's fists in the full extension of each of our foremost, initial punches. We then began to exchange elbows, knees, swinging backfists, all the while dodging and blocking each other's strikes with the tiniest of nanometers, for each of us, were, after all, in this moment, the two single greatest and formidable fighters in all of history.

Our hand-to-hand fight eventually stalemated, for we had been connecting all of our blows with each of our guards, and despite the rapidness of our exchanges, we had done minimal damage to each other. I then saw that Satan stepped back, having dodged one of my roundhouse kicks with a backwards bending spinal maneuver, and he looked at me, with his perfectly pale porcelain skin, that resembled a vampire chiseled out of marble, the sheer perfection of his appearance was most certainly worthy of the moniker: Vessel of Satan.

"I'm having fun, yourself?", Satan then barked at me, expressing his pleasantness at our exchanging of physical prowess, but it was then that I saw he had changed his posture, from the several meters he was away from me, and he assumed more of a street-fighter pose, with his arms front in center of his body, covering his face, and with his arms being locked into right degree angles, for it was the fighting stance of a boxer, a professional boxer, a true pugilist.

Satan had then, in all his aura of Sin, summoned upon himself every unfair street fight that had ever occurred, every mugging and robbery which resulted in the maiming of human life, every knockout punch to however many unmatched drunkards from an indignant club or bar bouncer that had ever transpired, for yes, he had abandoned the sanctity and prestige of the combined schools of martial arts, no, he was now a beast, a street fighter, fighting uncontrollably, and with unabashed wrathfulness.

I bobbed my head side to side, dodging his every strike, and his arms shot out like the break of a rubber band at full stretch, with the booming of elasticity, the thunderous snapping, and I returned my own strikes and blows, which he, at this point, decided to then eat, and bear the full brunt of, refusing to deflect or dodge, for he was on the full offensive, a true savage.

He then headbutted me, which did not phase me whatsoever, and I headbutted him back, immediately, and a single crack in his porcelain-like forehead then appeared, which then quickly healed.

Recognizing that this weaponless portion of our duel was going nowhere, he then shot upward, flying and raising himself against gravity to a terrifically high point in the sky, overlooking me, and the rest of our displaced, destroyed battleground, and he summoned upon him the power of telekinesis, a lost art once taught by the Fallen Angels themselves, and he then pulled with a momentous amount of telekinetic force a total of fifteen large blocks of ice, from under the tundra's surface. These fifteen, multi-ton weighing blocks of ice were then circling him, orbiting his aura of Sin, his blood red energetic charge which radiated from his body's aura, and I thought to myself, perhaps the fifteen blocks represented Nero's birthdate, which was on the fifteenth.

Satan looked down at me with much pride, having exalted himself both figuratively, and literally, and he announced sadistically, "As my little pawn once said, catch."

Once by one, the fifteen blocks of ice, more resembling of that of literal meteors, than anything, flew towards me, and with the grace of what these humans had developed in the recent years, with their cyber-ninja suits, I stepped and propelled myself like a torpedo, dodging each and every single one of them in a manner that only the most svelte and deliberate of ballet dancers, that had ever lived, could appreciate.

As I let the final boulders of ice miss me, having smashed into the snowy ground, displacing mountains of snow and ice, it had occurred to me, that I had let this transpire for far too long, this encounter had to come to an end, so that I could save Naydyr, my friend, one of my dearest and closest children, who was so terribly broken inside, who needed my love, my affection, my presence, and it pained me, it bothered me, to think what Satan was subjecting him to, what experience he was having in Hell, in Satan's place, and I had made my decision, Satan's time on earth was up.

Satan, had, quite interestingly, planned to defeat me, and then to rule the planet earth, which had been mostly scorched in nuclear annihilation, with the heart of the People's Soviet Empire being his personal throne, which then would lead to the enslavement of all remaining humans on earth, and the unleashing of literal demons, through dark energy portals, essentially ushering in Hell on earth. Yes, this was his perverse plan, which he had used Naydyr to execute so far, but no more, no more insanity, this was to be finished, now, and forever.

And thus, like my namesake as the Light of the World, as the Redeeming Light of God, I then materialized in front of Satan at the very speed of light, instantaneously, and his shocked face amused me, and I know that it amused the Saints, and the other spirits who were watching. It was then that I placed my right hand on his left shoulder. And from my mouth, came the Breath of the Lord, and I breathed unto him a great wind, an overpowering gust of air, which then, invisibly, completely renounced and removed Satan's reddish soul essence from that of Naydyr's golden yellow soul, reclaiming Naydyr's body for himself, although, this would be a gradual process, and he would have to be welcomed back, by my own efforts, to save him from Hell.

In Naydyr's face then, it was apparent, for the Satanic influence was being drained from him, seemingly ounce by ounce, and the demonic scowl which strew itself across his visage metamorphosed into a sleepful expression, for Naydyr's body was then comparable to a husk, momentarily, as Naydyr's reclamation of his own vessel had just started, and was not complete, just yet.

I must admit, that if it seemed as if I disposed of Satan rather casually, it's because it was, rather admittedly, something I could've done from the very beginning. For Satan was a being, a consciousness, an entity, that was significantly and notably less powerful than myself, and he always had been, and always would be, and the battle that had just transpired was no different. I had felt the urge, or inclination, to let him have some fun of his own, so that my precious people at Payurov Military Base could observe a spectacle, a lightshow, a demonstration of divine and ungodly powers altogether. I had let him feel as if he had a chance to win, which he never truthfully did. Interestingly enough, Satan had made a great risk for himself, coming into this physical plane, for he put himself at risk of being destroyed more severely than he had ever risked before, for he was imitating what our Father had exercised with me, using a physical human host for himself to fill in. And when he had come into this host, he had restrained himself to the constraints of this mortal plane, despite being an immortal being of evil, he had created a new set of parameters that he exposed himself to, being the rules and laws of nature in this reality, for before, he did not exist in this reality, but rather the esoteric, transcendental realm, and Sesto was just a flimsy illusion, not the true physical avatar that was Naydyr's body. It was, in an ironic and equally poetic way, an inverse of my original life on earth, where I had let the Father be born as myself, and I had let myself be crucified, and died, and my essence then departed from this world, having risen to heaven. And in direct parallel perversion, Satan had come into Naydyr's body, and just as quickly, departed from this world, having been sent back to Hell.

My power is immeasurable, the scope of my influence is incalculable, my energy is untamable, for I am the Alpha, and the Omega, and I have seen the end, and I shall live forever more. Satan had held, quite literally, no candle to my prowess whatsoever. Our confrontation was equivalent to an adult parent letting their child throw a temper tantrum, only to put them in time out for five minutes, and then put them to sleep. And just like that, with the slightest of ease, I had erased Satan from this plane of existence, and he was sent back to Hell, where he would have no hope of ever returning to Earth, not in a physical host, ever again.

I did not even allow him any final last words, before I banished him to nothingness. He did not deserve it, for he had misguided one of my sheep so heavily, and so regrettably, and so heartbreakingly, I could not, even in my infinite grace and forgiveness, even spare him any semblance of a farewell, any trace of any sort of honorable sendoff.

This was because I was to now establish my Kingdom of Heaven on Earth, as the holy scriptures had prophesied, which my mind was then focused on, for I had already cast away that unsavory encounter, with that accursed serpent, that Red Dragon, that accuser.

And thus, a new era on earth, and in history, had just begun.

It was then that I released the protective force field surrounding my precious people, my beloved sheep, being the now defunct People's Soviet Empire's soldiers, and the brave Western heroes and the oh so special French heroine, and even Ruslan, who at this point, was then accepted by his brothers, for he had witnessed the very culmination of history, and he had understood the error of his heart, and he had changed his beliefs, for he had seen and understood God's saving and forgiving grace, my grace.

After I had released the force field, I then flew up into the sky, up into the upper atmosphere of the earth, and I summoned a flute into my hands, and I began to play a smooth, relaxing, holy, welcoming and wondrous jazz melody, for jazz was one of my favorite creations of the modern man, which I appreciated greatly, and had a heartfelt appreciation for, being the free-flowing, cooperative and harmonious nature of it, which reminded me of water.

Emanating from this flute I then played was a phosphorus light, a blinding white phenomenon, that then radiated in full circumference from myself, having started to expand from my very position above Siberia to all reaches of the world, to all the scorched ruins and decimated cities that once stood tall and proud as a testament to mankind's civilizing effort. From my mouth came the Breath of the Lord, which I harnessed and focused into my flute, and it spread to all the burning fields and acres of farmland that had been permanently ruined by nuclear fallout and radiation, and to all the dilapidated forests and vegetation, which many of which had been staples of this earth for thousands of years, having grown and grown, harboring life and ecosystems, my white light then covered all of it, encapsulating it all in healing energy. All the deceased and mangled bodies, which numbered in the many billions, which tore at my heart, and brought a tear to my eye, to see such senseless tragedy, I then covered them each in my white healing light as well. From my flute I played a song of regeneration, a song of relief, and alleviation, and it functioned as the warm embrace of a mother for their newborn baby, for there could be no greater love, and it was the same love, the love of the Father, that I spread all throughout the earth, for everyone was to be saved, everyone was to be brought back alive, to live again, to walk in my Kingdom, and walk in my name, the name of the Lord. Even the infants, and the children, who had perished in nuclear fire, for I shed another tear, having seeing them through the lens of my white phosphorous, and I covered them, enwrapping them in my love, having then mitigated their wounds, and their burns, on a cellular, molecular level, and they were healing. For may I not forget, the elderly, and the seniors, those of old age, who were feeble, and meek, who had succumbed to the brute force and savagery of sheer unparalleled destruction, from my flute I then breathed pure life unto them, unto their bodies, their ever-so disrespected vessels, and they had begun to heal as well. And lest I not forget the animals, the truest obedient servants of our Father, who fell prey and victim to the betrayal of the human race, and all the birds who had fallen and littered the streets and parkways, for they were covered in my white phosphorous, and all the cows and pigs, and horses and elephants, monkeys and even the creatures of the seas, every single one, they were all enveloped in my saving grace, the white, abounding light which sourced from my flute's end. And I shed another tear, for the horses, for who had only ever served their masters with utmost dedication, all throughout history, and especially the dogs and cats, who had only ever been loyal friends and companions to their masters, and whom were betrayed, as well, by mankind, for I shed a tear for them all, and I swathed and blanketed their smoldered carcasses, and they had begun to heal, too.

It was then that the tears I had shed from my face, they then dripped down from this upper atmosphere and fell to the earth, and this water which had come from myself, it then spawned a whole new host of vegetation and foliage that then began to spread across the scarred earth, and pockets of greenery, and trees, and vines, and bushes all had begun to grow, and mature, and establish themselves upon the surface of the earth, and their roots dug deep into the inner levels of the dirt of the earth, and they had born anew, from the devastating reset of nuclear holocaust, a luscious and bountiful harvest, a new face to the earth. For plants, vegetables, flora, and all the like, they too were alive, and in the noblest of existences, they could not exert their influence forcibly upon their external elements, like humans and animals, for they were rooted, and non-moving, and they, too, had been so terribly and regrettably abused by humanity, so betrayed, and I had brought them again a new life, a new generation of persistent opportunity to then blossom again, to spread their seeds, grow their fruits and vegetables, and they, too, were healed and born again.

With the people of earth, and the animals of earth, and lastly the vegetation of earth, all healed and resurrected, for it had been written, in the scriptures, that I would return, and breath new life into the world, and these three categories, representative of the trinity on this physical plane, had been made right again, and the earth was now a paradise, a newly born playground of boundless food and limitless resources, and it had represented the once archaic and primordial Garden of Eden.

My people, my sheep of my flock, they then raised themselves out of the ashes of the bombings, which had now dissipated into nothingness, for it had been overwritten and done away with from the white phosphorous, and they leaped and shouted, they jumped in joy and limitless happiness, for they knew they had been given the gift of life once again, and their former fate of ruthless death was done away with and defeated, and they could tell, they were together again, with their wives and sons and daughters and brothers and sisters, and they hugged, and kissed, and cried, and laughed, and they knew, within their hearts, that this was now a world of no more sickness, no more inequality, or iniquity, or injustice, for they were all kings and queens and divine royalty in their own right, they had been kissed with the loving embrace of the Father, and they lived, again.

I then lowered myself to the earth's lower atmosphere, and then lower to the visible sky, and I had materialized a space out of the canopies and verdure, luscious greenery, and I had fashioned a throne for myself, a physical seating for myself to then descend to, and it was raised, and elevated enough to be seen for miles, a great distance, and I was met with singing, and awe-inspiring, joyous praise, from all the resurrected peoples of the world, and the entire world was unified, and together, at long last.

It was all perfect, then, and I smiled to myself in satisfaction, and happiness. I knew then that I had fulfilled my mission, as ordained by the Father, and as so cleverly predicted and prophesied by the authors of the book, the Holy Book. And I chuckled to myself, for I had waited for this moment for much a great deal of time, inconceivable to any human, and it had arrived, my homecoming, my entrance to the earth, and it was more visceral and wonderful of an experience for even myself, and my smile grew to a complete and utter beaming grin, for I had righted the wrongs and errors of humanity, and forgiven them, even still, and gifted them with the

Kingdom of Heaven on Earth, for that's what it was.

But it was not wholly complete, no, not yet, while although it was perfect and without any flaw, it was not complete, no, it was not.

For my dearest and most lost sheep, my most tried and tribulated, and harmed and most needing of my love, of the Father's love, for he was not here yet, he was not yet here, with us, with the rest of his brothers and sisters, and fellow humans.

No, he was still separated, still in the dark, still lost and so heartbreakingly denying of my embrace, still without my earnest companionship, my guidance, and counseling, he was still stuck in Hell, yes, he was so far from the rest of us, he was not with us, and this pained me.

He had not yet seen the sheer inspiring glory of my new earth, and it was true, yes, for so poetically, and ironically, and tragically, yes, he would be the very last person to be welcomed to the Kingdom of Heaven on Earth, for he was that special, he was that most deserving of this additional care and attention, his journey had been unlike anyone else's ever in history, and he had followed the beat of his own drum, vainly so.

I loved him, and I needed him with me, with the rest of us.

He had an iconic name, a legendary name that inspired awe and wonder, and fear alike, in the hearts and minds of his fellow members of humanity.

And I would then come and get him.

I would save him.

My dearest child.

Naydyr Chanming.

CHAPTER 10

I Love You

God's Saving Grace

God's Loving Embrace

"Do you love me...?", he muttered.

"Always have, always will", I said.

...

...

"Do you forgive me...?", he whimpered.

"Only if you forgive yourself", I said.

...

...

This short but forebodingly telling and heavy exchange then flashed across Naydyr's mind, but as soon as it flashed, it then exited the inner-workings of his mind just as quickly. It was like a flash in a pan, like a lightning bolt that came and went.

He then turned around, to see what hand was placed on his left shoulder, for the hand that had touched him then recoiled away, and pulled back, and as soon as he turned around to see, his vision went pitch black, and he could not make out anything, and the dark, tormenting heat of Hell was then quickly replaced with a cooling, misty, clean aroma, that he felt was alleviating the heat he had felt, in his time in Hell.

In this pitch black, he then felt himself lift off the ground, off the floor of what was once the Lowest Echelon of Hell's firmament, and he began to float up, into the darkness, which he then floated up as if he was in an open sea, but he could then breathe water effortlessly, so it wasn't really like a sea, all that much, but that was the closest his mind could relate the sensation to.

Eventually, he felt a ground underneath him, and plopped and landed on it softly.

He then saw, in the dark, a spotlight had turned on, from what looked like a ceiling light, not unlike the ceiling lights that had haunted him from his American boarding schools he attended in his youth, which he despised.

But in his heart, he could not despise anything, any more. He no longer held onto any resentment of any kind, for anything.

He felt isolated, and alone. And he missed Nero terribly, who he had grown accustomed to talking to all day, every day, for a majority of his life at that point, before he had been sent to Hell.

Going to Hell changes a man. And Naydyr, in all his special titles and honorifics and the like, was, after all, just another man, before our Father.

Underneath this spotlight then walked into the light, directly under it, a small, petite figure.

It was Naydyr as a little boy. A little, inconspicuous, harmless, innocent, yet already a genius prodigy at many things, little eleven-year-old Naydyr.

At that point in Naydyr's life, he still adorned the last name of his Russian father, Lachashev. This period of Naydyr's young life where he was still referred to as, "Naydyr Lachashev", was a harkening to his past life as Nero, where Nero was not known as "Nero" just yet, but rather by his original birth name, "Lucius". For when the harsh and strict, domineering American boarding school teachers and disciplinarians at his junior boarding school for children referred to him as "Lachashev", they were, in a recycling of energy, mimicking how Nero was called "Lucius" in his youth.

Anyways, Naydyr then looked at his younger self, who looked back at him. His eleven-year-old self was also wearing his same school uniform, and was staring at him blankly, with a deadpan expression.

Naydyr then broke down, and was crying, profusely. He fell to his very knees, he had crumpled under his own weight, with his right hand covering his eyes, wiping away the tears. He couldn't even bring himself to look back at his eleven-year-old self, he was so ashamed, so disappointed in the squandering of his boundless, infinite potential he had held at that age, how he could've been anything in the world other than the damnable monster he had become, what he had deliberately chosen to devolve into. Having looked upon the innocent face of himself at eleven, he recognized the trajectory he had delved and nosedived into, being his fascination with the occult, and demons, and dark magic, which he now recognized as so terribly perverse and offensive to God, having just been sent to Hell itself. He remembered how he had functioned more comparable to that of a political entrepreneur, rather than a true, noble politician of the people he represented, always seeking to empower and embolden himself through a myriad of twisted and corrupt opportunities, and how he had fallen short in that regard as well. He, then, with all the regret in his soul, and his heart, then let out a wail of pure and pitiful pain, for he then also remembered all the very children he had so casually chosen to annihilate!

The little eleven-year-old Naydyr then walked up closer to him, and then Naydyr himself looked up at his younger self, from his crumpled state, meeting his gaze yet again, and the young Naydyr then spoke, and said, in a voice which was one-to-one with the real young Naydyr, saying, "You know, I think you're pretty cool. I would have never thought I'd grow up to be so important and powerful. That stuff's pretty cool."

Before the shocked Naydyr could react, the young boy then smirked, and the spotlight above him shut off, abruptly. The little boy had disappeared, and there was no trace of him. He had vanished out of thin air.

Naydyr then composed himself, and stood up, having wiped away the last of his tears. It then occurred to himself, that he had quite a lot to be proud of, albeit despite his tarnished reputation before God, he was still remarkably influential and unique in all of history. He had, as the little boy said, become the single most "powerful" and "important" man who ever lived, by any and all accounts, biased or unbiased, for it was impossible to ignore the facts of his actions, his swaying speeches, and his sweeping reforms across all of Eurasia.

No, he wasn't worthless.

He wasn't a failure.

He was amazing. He had faltered, in the end, and maybe more honestly towards a majority of the time leading up to the end, but he still had achieved so much. He knew that his teachers and instructors and disciplinarians in which he despised and hated for always telling him what to do, he knew they were proud of him, truly, that they held with pride the badge of once being a figure in the young life of the fabled Naydyr Chanming, the once little Lachahsev.

He still felt awful, but he felt better about himself.

It was then that, out of the darkness, spawned another spotlight, and into it walked someone he was not prepared to see, someone who struck a nerve even harsher and more personal than even that of his eleven-year-old self.

Pei.

It was his one and only wife, which he had married, who had been his on-and-off lover all throughout his adult life, it was who he once called his "soulmate", yes, it was Pei Peizhi, who was dressed in an outfit she would've worn on any given regular, run-of-the-mill day that Naydyr may have spent in his personal palace which he shared with her, for when he wasn't out and about, traveling.

She walked right up to him, and the emotions were too much for him to handle, the sudden rush of endorphins coursing all throughout his body, having paralyzed him under his own grief, he then looked away from her face, to his left, putting both palms over his face, in a defeated pose, having been too embarrassed to look at the woman he had once promised to that he would save the world. He had thought to himself, in that instant, how he had become so awfully distant to her, how inconsiderably neglectful, how poor of a husband, a life partner, to her, that he leaned into being towards the latter stages of World War III. He had thought how he spent so many months and years away from his wife, who loved and appreciated him with every ounce of her being, and how he never even gave her children to love, to take care of, for he was too busy, too preoccupied with chasing power, too in love with his own legacy and not his own wife, no, he was an awful husband, he was the worst, he ought to be ashamed, and to be before her, in all his vulnerability, he wailed again, in pain, for he could not burden the failure that he felt in his very bones, for he was failure personified, he was failure incarnate.

Pei then stepped to him, coming closer, and she said to him, "I was so proud to be your wife. You made me the proudest woman who ever lived, all the fame and attention you brought to me, to my career. And there was simply no debate, there was never a man I had ever met who was more beautiful, than you, more intelligent, than you, more well-read and well-spoken, than you, more dedicated to his work, than you. You were so brilliantly perfect in so many ways, too many ways to count. I loved you more than I loved myself, and you did so much for me. I'll always love you, my perfect, handsome superman."

And then just like that, the spotlight went out, and she had removed herself from his presence, she had vanished, just like the younger Naydyr had.

Naydyr then felt a rush of even more emotion overpower him, and he stood up, straightening himself out, rubbing his eyes, rubbing the tear imprints from his face. He reasoned to himself... maybe it was true, maybe he was a great husband after all. He knew that he was responsible for her musical career. He knew that, most definitely, no other man on earth held a candle to what he could provide for her, the protection he could offer her, the status and prestige that came with being his wife, his closest confidant. He felt better, then, that he was reassured, yes, that he was a good husband, an acceptable husband, someone his wife was proud to have married. He also knew, which he had forgotten, for it came so naturally and effortlessly to him, so second-nature to him, that he had always remained loyal to her, that not once did he ever cheat on her, or was he ever unfaithful to her.

He felt better. He knew he was a good husband, after thinking about it for a second, after hearing her words, he knew, then, that perhaps in being so conscious of the standard that he held himself to, he had lost grip with reality, with what really was the case, what really was the truth.

Then, all of a sudden, another spotlight came on, with this one being the biggest and the brightest of all three.

A sudden chill went down Naydyr's spine then. He was curious who he would encounter next, who from his life would appear before him, this time.

This next time, he was stronger, stronger than he had been previously, he was more confident in himself, he had told himself, "Ok, I am done crying."

And then, someone with his exact height, weight, and stature, had then pronouncedly and confidently strolled into the light. This person that had stepped into the light was staring straight into Naydyr's deepest depths of his soul, for it was as if they were looking through him, and into him, into his deepest insecurities and vulnerabilities, and any and all caveats to his personality and ego. This figure was also wearing a beautifully gorgeous and ornate apparel, for it was a brilliantly passionate red and royalty-invoking purple tunic and robe, stretching and wrapped across his body, which was then decorated and dressed with golden embroideries.

It was 666 himself.

Nero Caesar.

Nero.

In the flesh.

Naydyr's jaw dropped to the floor, he could not fathom what his eyes were comprehending. In a then uncontrollable impulse, he lunged forward with all his might and wrapped both his arms around Nero's upper body, having embraced him in a forcible hug, and he had sunk his face into Nero's chest, and bawled his eyes out, sobbing and sniveling to no end. He could not even think of what to say, for he had missed Nero so much, so heart wrenchingly, his banter and companionship, and he began to hyperventilate, like that of someone crying unabashedly and uncontrollably, incapable of formulating any words, any approximation of what he wished to say, which was how much he missed him.

Nero then shed a single tear of his own, which trailed down from his right cheek. He took his right hand and placed it on Naydyr's head, caressing his hair, in an expression of comforting him, and he smiled to himself. Yes, it was true, Nero had dreamed of this moment for ages, the moment he would be able to physically interact with his future incarnation, it was just as emotional for him as it was for Naydyr, but he knew he had to be stronger, he had to be the bigger brother, the guide, and wise teacher that he always had been for him, for a majority of his life.

Nero then leaned his head forward, with Naydyr still sobbing copiously, closer to Naydyr's face, and he whispered into his ear, speaking softly and comfortingly, "Shh, shh, my dearest brother, my champion, my hero, my greatest friend who ever was. I know I had to leave you, for a short time, and I'm deeply sorry. You've been so strong, my friend. So incredibly strong. Stronger than I ever could've hoped to be. It's okay now, you're with me again. I'm here."

Nero continued to pet Naydyr's hair, and he continued comforting him, saying, "I love you; you know? The life you lived was the greatest spectacle of all ages, you did it bigger than me, and that's being generous to me. You were a true superstar, and you don't have to suffer anymore, you don't have to fight anymore, because I know that's what you are, friend, that's what we both are, fighters, fighting everything in this world that misunderstands us, that hurts us, that labels and antagonizes us. But through it all, you persevered so brilliantly. You had the hardest job, out of all us, only you, only you, Naydyr, could have done all this, could have done what was necessary. You were the strongest who ever lived. You made me so proud, and I won't be leaving you again, Naydyr."

Naydyr then raised his face, having put his chin up, and he locked eyes with his past life, Nero, and he had no idea, that this moment was considered the greatest and most special privilege before our Father that any mortal could ever be bestowed, that was, to meet your past life in a physical setting, individual to individual, for past lives and future lives were never intended nor meant to co-exist simultaneously, in a physical capacity, for that constructed a very tricky scenario, an unnatural one. For once a person's life on earth is over, they are then meant to depart from tangibility, and are tasked with designing and laying out the life of their next life, their next incarnation, and this was the order and progression of the soul that our Father had intended for us.

"You're more handsome than me, Nero", Naydyr had finally spoken, having found the courage to finally talk, and he was now smiling ear to ear, looking straight into Nero's eyes, who was looking straight back at him, smiling as well.

"I love you, brother", Nero then said back, and his eyes began to water up, for he was about to cry too.

But before Naydyr could react, Nero then put his left hand over Naydyr's chest, and in a sudden instant, the spotlight above them shut off, and Naydyr felt Nero absorb back into him, back into his seat of consciousness, and he realized, just how exclusively special and meaningful this short, tangible encounter was, with his past life. Having then felt a whirlwind of warm energy spiraling into his heart, his soul, and having Nero back inside him, Nero then quickly communicated to him that he had deliberately lied to him, at his wedding, that Sesto was Cupid, because it was up to Naydyr to figure this out for himself, and he couldn't give him all the answers, all the cheats. Nero then even more so quickly elaborated how through his villainy, he had united the whole world, against him, but it by this unification that it was essential to God's plan for the world. And Nero, being the earnest, failed artist that he so fervently wished he could've been, had then designed Naydyr's life as his ultimate art piece, his ultimate tragedy and work of beauty that ever was.

The black darkness around Naydyr then drained away, along with Nero having dissipated into Naydyr's heart, and it was actually the blackness of Nero's soul that was perpetuating this veil of darkness.

Nero, after all, was the Italian word for the color

black.

Once this blackness had finished disappearing, Naydyr then saw that he was in a paradise, a paradise beyond his wildest comprehension.

Ruslan then ran over to Naydyr, and so did Joan, and Raven, and Alaric, and Henry, and all the former soldiers.

In these people's hearts, there were no hints of revenge, or vengeance, or grudging animosity towards him, like he expected.

No, in their hearts now lie only the yearning to mend, and forgive, and heal, and love.

Everything had worked out, perfectly, in the end.

There were many twists, and periods of uncertainty, in the Tribulation that had now passed, but in the end, the beauty of it all was evident.

For how could anyone conceivably hold a grudge when all was right, all was perfect with the world, at that point, and it had become apparent, that everything had happened for a reason, that all the pain and loss were only lessons, to better appreciate and understand the importance and perfection of what life was now like.

And it was understood that Naydyr had been tasked with the hardest of tasks, the most difficult of roles to play in this, this new perfection of the world, for only he could have done the things he did, oh how genius God was, it was all a part of his divine plan.

Naydyr and Ruslan hugged, and cried.

Joy smiled at Naydyr, and Naydyr smiled back.

Raven shook Naydyr's hand.

Alaric and Henry both nodded in respect towards him.

It was complete, then.

They all then danced around.

They all laughed.

It was beautiful.

It was perfect.

ABOUT THE AUTHOR

Noah Hewitt

Noah is a young man in his early twenties from America. He is passionate about storytelling, compelling characters, and art that evokes an emotional response. Much of his inspiration comes from history and religion. Music, movies, television, and videogames also stir his creativity. Noah hopes to impart wisdom and expressiveness to his readers. Anyone at all who may lend their ear to what he has to say. He currently resides in America.

EPILOGUE

What appeared wrong turned out to still be wrong but a lesson and chance to render something the most right and best afterall in the end too. Mainly everyone after the fact all agreed. Lyric Abdiel was not forgotten. He was brought back too along with everyone else. Naydyr learned to pray.

AFTERWORD

Even if many religions and philosophies aren't believable to you, still learn about them. In disagreeing you further distinct what you agree with. What people thought happens after death is a belief not to do with religion or philosophy really. Every child wonders that themselves already. Perhaps, religion and philosophy were born with just a child, not the prophet or thinker. I've never heard that ever said. And how can a child have caused wars and empires? Simple. The child knows truest, they only know what they know. Untainted by others yet. Of course, what's truest renders what's greatest. Institutions that have survived for thousands of years always have some degree of merit to them. Not because they were all true, but that they reflected what people said to each other. What people did to each other. That is all that has ever happened, someone affecting someone else. Life is really much more literal than many ever realize. What someone did someone witnessed to remember to tell someone else who persisted the past into the future.

ACKNOWLEDGEMENT

Thank you God for giving me the ultimate chance that's life. Especially that particular year I happend to be born. What a special time I'm alive in! Thank you Mom for having always made me breakfast. All the other blessings too. My truest supporter from even before the start.

www.ingramcontent.com/pod-product-compliance
Lightning Source LLC
Chambersburg PA
CBHW072150170626
46813CB00004BA/1754